ANIMAL TALES

ANIMAL TALES

JOHN FRASER

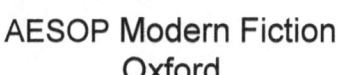

AESOP Modern Fiction
Oxford

AESOP Modern Fiction
An imprint of AESOP Publications
Martin Noble Editorial / AESOP
28 Abberbury Road, Oxford OX4 4ES, UK
www.aesopbooks.com

First hardback edition published by AESOP Publications
Copyright (c) 2014 John Fraser
First paperback edition published by AESOP Publications
Copyright (c) 2014 John Fraser

www.johnfraser.info

ISBN: 978-0-9927588-4-4

Contents

ANIMAL TALES

'... il serra sa tortue sous son manteau qui lui paraissait cacher vraiment tout ce qu'il y avait d'exceptionnel au monde.'

Jules Supervielle, *Le voleur d'enfants* (1926)

Collecting

'We're getting a reputation among Muslims. Buddhists too,' Gill says.

'We don't want to be known for welcoming groups. We shouldn't use that as criterion, that "we want a few of you for a quota".' That's Peter.

'We don't want to end with some minority taking us over. Or them opening the doors and being a majority.'

'Let everyone come, and metamorphise. Or not, as they wish. I hate groups, people niggling each other to be the same,' Peter says.

'Everyone wants people to agree with them,' says Gill. 'That's the end of philosophy, religion – all the values must be sorted out. Then they're self-evident. You can't not follow the self-evident. So you're either on the boat, or drowning in the water. Even if you only barely believe that a boat can give you a better chance.'

Peter and Gill, they chatter on about admissions.

'In the end, we take the interesting few. It's original every time,' says Peter.

'No, my dear,' says Gill, 'It's Proust! And none the worse.'

'Do we do this because we're rich, or because we're poor?' Peter asks.

'It's a new colonialism – taking guys and their tradition, making them cosmopolitans,' says Gill, doubtfully.

'We're all colonials, and all cosmopolitans. It's a pain. It's what we want,' says Peter.

'I don't want it. But I don't know how to say I don't,' says Gill.

Peter and Gill, their creative studies group they call a college, a foundation. Filled with Fellows, come from everywhere, each with a plan, each wanting to make the world believe in them. Gill sees me in the anteroom, listening through the open door. 'This guy,' he says about me, 'Would you believe his dad's so stupid – he's in a federal jail. He brought his things over the state line, because he didn't know it ran right through his house!'

Anyone can make a lie like that, we're full of similar, everyone.

Each week the creatives and the politicos hash up a plot. It's lunch. Nadia here – makes the arty pies they eat. She ought to get a prize for them. Eatart.

I used to be an interesting guy, they took me so, and at once – I wasn't.

Gill won't let go: 'This guy,' he tells Peter, 'used to

play for the Chicago Bulls.'

I can't skate. I keep schtum.

'You could wait on tables,' Peter says, 'It's really "wait on us", but you keep it impersonal.'

Gill asks, 'How's your project? What was it again?'

I improvise: 'Fantastic animals.'

'That's orientalist,' says Gill.

'There's centaurs,' I say: 'And Leda. And Europa. Of course, there's the simurgh, and the Prophet's flying donkey. And princely monkeys. Dragons, gryphons, cockatrices. Snakes. The roc.'

'It's all sex,' says Gill.

'I hadn't thought of that,' I say. 'They're just cute. It's the imagination. Then there's Ganesh. You can't put gods in among the animals – and yet, they're all mixed up in it.'

'Your categories are mixed in any case,' says Peter, disappointed: 'You've just a box of tricks.'

These guys act as if they're rich. They just administer huge sums.

*

Gill makes to leave. I think I'll line his hand in the door and try to pin it. Instead, he takes off stooping, and I get to close the door on the top part of his skull. It brings tears to his face, but he smiles at me. Does he mean – 'try to be nicer?' Or – 'I'll try not to provoke?' Or it's just perverse. Maybe he likes it, what he was hoping for. There's silence,

Peter makes like the chorus in Wozzeck. 'Poor man,' his body says, and I can't pretend to apologise. 'Poor man,' that's it, that's all.

All this enlightenment – it's all for investment opportunities. Where to site the gallery, histories of awkward places. Deep into religions – underneath, it's where refined guys feel safe to lay down cash.

If only Nadia didn't stake her life upon her pies and tarts – 'Don't eat that!' she shouts. 'I put cement dust in, to make it last for ever,' as I try a piece. We'd last for ever, some relationship – that's what they're called – if she hadn't hitched herself to beauty. 'You're interesting,' Nadia says to me, 'because you're empty. That's what Peter says. You're a jar. You must be hollow. What might we put into you?'

'Emptiness is good,' I say to Nadia: 'It's what you always start with. At the end, there's always scruffy scuts and such.'

Gill's head is tall and creased, in bright colours. We should all practise head-binding – once, it showed the winning lineage. Another fantasy, a brilliant bird, comes to my mind – the Garuda, venerable, and venerated.

Peter makes a speech to all the patrons: collectors, real estate guys, the simply rich. New good things depart, he says, flag and fame will follow after, quickly. Shows for glass cases, shows carried on the backs of animals, shows ethereal and stuck with glue. The buildings. Transfers of everything, including hope.

'No!' I shout, 'that isn't new. Things really new –

they bring poverty, oppression. Bitter food, forbidden drink. The bosses – monsters, superficial, cruel, obsessive. The new means jail, my friends, discipline and music ultraloud for you, confiscation of everything, your wives and kids taken from your record, sent off to wander, dying on the treks and in the camps. Buildings unpainted, thronged with desperate nameless guys who'll steal your bed; the grass to eat, the rain to drink, the lathe to worship all day long. Nights, too. New litanies to learn, new guys to touch your forelock to ... that's what the new is all about, until it falls, and then more new will come, always the same. What you have here is not the new, it's middle journey stuff ... old cash, the old machines now speeded up, a jolt of volts, and faster on you spin. It's not the new. It is the old that dies, there's terror, then there's terror, multiplied, renewed.'

'How could you? How dare you tell them that?' asks Nadia. 'They can see it, if they want. These cakes, my beauties – one day they'll be dust, inedible. It's all there, if you want to know your destiny. To see it, hurts, it costs. Maybe these guys here – prefer that it's just interesting?'

'Who understands that?' I ask. 'It's just a classic spiel about the ending up. They take it as a spur to carry on.'

'You piece of grit,' shouts Peter. 'Grit in the shoes. Grit in the eye. No – big grit in the bladder. You bastard!'

Gill says, 'Peter is upset, you know.'

'Observations, I make, not conclusions,' I say.

'Not upset concerned, upset angry,' Gill says. His head is like a fire.

He goes on, 'It's your nihilism, when we've nothing but good will.'

There is much more from Gill.

'Here, touch it. For luck,' says Nadia.

'What's this?' I ask. It's a dusty clay bulb.

'A cake,' she says, shyly: 'It's a cat's scrotum.'

'It ought to be in silver,' I say.

'Maybe I'll try metals next,' she says: 'I'll go on. My pace, of course. But – you're in trouble here. Are they letting you go?'

'Oh, I'll expel myself,' I say, 'like an owl's pellet. Those two – they're liberals. They don't like things happening suddenly. They like that things should last long times.'

Nadia's a good girl, good for what – you shouldn't think it.

As I go down the marble steps, there pops into my mind – 'Chimera!'

'You're so reactionary!' Nadia says.

I say, 'No, I want the new to come, terrible, fearful; it brings soldiers in wooden boots, the heels of brass. They splinter everything.'

Gill says to me, 'You'll not amount to something. You are a primitive, we'll find your bones scattered across the plain a hundred years from now. Nameless. Nameless, unlamented, like the massive quantity of others, disarticulated bones. But – here comes the bargain! We can expel you, but we'd rather keep you humbly on. We are the gatekeepers – at our backs the treasure. You can guard the door. A porter. You have no access – you stand upon the access. In and out they go – and you stay there, on the threshold, and you salute them as they come in, depart.'

'It sounds quite good,' I say, 'Not bad, at least.'

*

I stand at the door, letting them in, with cash, and out, without. In with a plan, out with a grant.

Each is an animal, fantastic – sometimes not. Here's a wealthy lady, one of those Russian chickens, from some witch's hut, nearly two metres tall.

Peter says to her, and points to me, 'This guy comes from a mountain village – they're all some nativist heresy. They don't talk in case their soul flies from their mouths – so! we don't know what language, if any, he can speak.' They stare, the lady – the tall chicken – looks alarmed, Peter goes on,

'Look at his baggy pants. That's how you tell. Where he comes from, it's too cold to try a new pair on. You take what comes. They've burnt the trees – we let those people in as charity.'

'Those pants,' she says. 'Can you be sure that's not the mode?'

'If you are poor,' says Gill, 'There's nothing but imagination. You must create and fantasise – that's what we take from them. It doesn't cost a cent.'

'No regrets,' says Peter: 'That's what you need. Or

don't need: regrets. No time, no place, no person: what you have is the best you'll have.'

I'm impressed: 'Peter! That's the sharpest thing you've said. Though it leaves you up there, and me on the door. The thing to be is deadpan. Where does that come from – deadpan? The cinema? Makeup? Gold-digging? A fry-up? You're right, Peter, "minding" about people – is a trap. Your dog got killed? There's others. Hear them barking to be let in. Your brother? Millions had that experience, more millions will – maybe you will too. We all come from a huge city with narrow alleys, where we love everyone and claw their eyes and suck their bones? Well, there's a heap of villages, with narrow alleys too...'

'That's not what I meant at all,' says Peter. 'I meant – no self-pity. No looking back, refusing justice to the bad guys, giving them some benefit. Besides, doormen aren't supposed to chat.'

'Everyone's a critic now, Peter,' says Marcia, the chicken lady: 'You do something, then you stand back, and it wasn't about you, but someone else. And some unconfessable coupling thrown in.'

Marcia is a fine person. Her knees, being scaly, do have that chicken look. But like most working people, quite poor, in this country, we live much of the time on dead chickens – nuggets, flightless wings and such, they're good to us.

Marcia was live, though, really live.

*

I say, 'Peter and Gill, and this circus – they want to rule the world.' Marcia says,

'I love Gill's head! The colours! That was clever of you. Rule the world? Of course they want that – so they do at Yale, Harvard, all those expensive systems. If they could, they'd all be there on stage, singing falsetto, making a music that gets you dancing, millions of you, forgetting what you were when you came in. So what? It doesn't happen.'

It's a new perspective: I say, 'I'm a harbourmaster. I don't carry things. That's what "porter" means. Like the Porte sublime. If you don't get by me, you don't get yes or no, nor a berth.'

'Are you sure about that?' asks Marcia. 'At any rate, someone or something rules the world, so while we're discussing and waiting – I'll tell you my solution. The next best thing to being top, but sure: collecting.'

I say, doubting, 'You and your man must have lots of cash. And when you're dead, your stuff flies off like dust.'

'Cash?' she says. 'You may pry, but that you cannot touch. Collecting stuff's the nearest to immortality. And nearest to that is mortality, of course, you silly boy. How could it be otherwise?

She has a fine mind, Marcia, and I feel I can ingratiate myself.

'Static and emotionless – that's the nature of your job,' says Marcia. 'It's Gill punishes you, forever on the door. Peter would have thrown you out. Always better to take the kick than the embrace.'

'Teach me, then, Marcia. You must have made a fortune, knowing things. Or cohabited with someone's gold,' I say.

'I have a little Sans Souci, that is true,' says Marcia. 'There, you could be a gatekeeper, not a concierge. Your job would still be to act as sceptic: who is in or out, how long do they stay, with whom. French exiles once did that work – now they're all resident, let everybody in, just gossip in the yard. I need a guy who'll keep intruders out. An outsider on the inside.'

'There!' says Nadia, 'I knew you'd get the cat's luck.'

I tell Marcia, 'Nadia sends you these Alice cakes.'

'Oh dear,' Marcia says, 'I'll put them up here, high, so they won't be seen, I mean, be eaten. I hope they won't make me change my size. They're not labelled ...'

'No one's ever tried them,' I say. 'That is the fun of it,' though Marcia's too tall as it is. Jeweller's enamel, hyperrealism – the cakes are made of that, so Nadia says, but—

'I don't want to hear about your love affair with Nadia,' Marcia says. 'We'll stick to Alice. Lots of fantastic animals in that, and chaste as well.'

'What's my job, Marcia?' I ask.

'First, I'll show you Hubert. He's called that now, after the saint – he used to love the hunt.'

There's a safe wall, that she unlocks. Inside, a frightened man. The suit is good. He's sweating, and Marcia says, 'It's for the money. They are after him. The capital's long gone, melted into artefacts.'

He could be Russian, or Chinese, or both, mixed with American. A fruity sundae on the melt. Marcia tells me, 'You mustn't think that I'm a Bluebeard in reverse. He is the only one, locked in the wall, locked in my heart.'

'Where's all the fancy stuff?' I ask. 'I guess I'm guarding it.'

There's copper cabinets, and cases bound with brass, the labels for or from Benares, Tallahassee and Noril'sk. 'The stuff is in museums,' Marcia says, 'Those are our power upon the past. We made our cash, the guys have sweated, quite like Hubert's doing now, and from necessity. Like him. Now all the collectibles are on display, not here. It's a contrition. Cash into ormolu – who has the best show, that's where the power lies—'

'So there is nothing here?' I interrupt. 'You gave it all away, like monks their potency, immunity, in knots tied in your belt?'

'Oh,' says Marcia, 'the people come to see the boxes that it went in, that's your task, to let them gawp,' and vaguely she flaps her hands. 'We have our flutes, of course.'

And there they are. Flutes – of tibias, of course, but every material is there – gourds and chalcedony, feldspar and zinc. And animals – you blow into the orifice – here's gods and goddesses: there is Minerva, Jupiter I see, platoons of Cupids, nymphs with fingerholes along their backs.

'Yes, that's all you need to do,' says Marcia, looking coy. 'Blow into them, but don't expect a melody. You see, everything gets recycled, into beauty. All the bad bosses, all their stuff ends up on our shelves – then into shows. How we love it! – axes, garrottes, see the patina, the craftsmanship ... The old machines.'

Marcia says, 'Peter and Gill – they both want Fellows. Good, and well met. Gill wants to send forth pilgrims. Journeying, poor, homesick, hoping for epiphany, then coming back to thank him. Peter wants saviours. They don't come back. They mostly end bad, who cares. They found new cultures. Peter is honoured, Gill remembered. You did bad to rough up Gill – Peter's the dangerous one.'

'But you gave them money, Marcia,' I say.

'Of course. Without money, vendetta doesn't last. I'm the avenger. In no one's name. Justice, perhaps. A shuffle of the cards. Those pilgrims – they shuffle round the exhibits. Do no harm. It's the crowing of the saviours, all their causes lost.'

'Yes, it's the pretension of it, Marcia,' I say, 'But you're quite pretentious too.'

'Don't be cheeky,' Marcia says, 'I can be cheeky, you can't. Remember where those cakes ended up.'

'Just leave them,' I say, 'your thoughts. And changing size.'

'No, no,' says Marcia, 'We're made like that, to pry and punish.'

'The guys you're looking for, on the top,' I say, 'They're bankers, experts, pros and such. The sump. Not the engine. You should look further.'

'I have a daughter,' Marcia says, 'But she's not for you.'

I can't think what to say: 'Our species – it has this tragedy before it, in its eyes – suicide, when it's killed all that's around it.'

She says, 'Hubert's dreams – he made them rule the lives of others. Of all who worked for him. Me too.'

'Of course,' I say. 'One has to have had parents. But where I come from – those narrow alleyways, the mountain villages, the big cities – you do things like you have to, like in a movie, the actors do what they can't do otherwise.'

'I can't believe you come from somewhere. A past,' she says. She doesn't think before she speaks. I say,

'People love it, the past, but not at the time, not when they're living it. Loving it: – to hate it wouldn't be intelligent. It's a punishment, for us. What you call independence, doing what you can afford to like – for us, it was a war, betrayals. Mine will always be a small place, full of people, lots falling back on being stupid. Poor people with no grasp, but lots of cling. Poor soils, nothing interesting you can do. For sure, we're going nowhere, we'll not be Indians, Chinese – puffed up.'

'Well,' she says, not taking all this in, 'That's why you'll stay a porter, unless you snap out of it.'

'Your daughter, Marcia, – is she shut up in a wall like Hubert?' I ask.

'No – if she were, it would be as treasure. Hubert's locked up for protection. And you, as bodyguard – you must prepare to die for him. That's the snag, in bodyguarding. The body is beautiful, you say you'd die for it, 'mother of God and hang me high!' – and then you have to!' She laughs.

'Hubert's the father, though, that I must die for?' I ask.

'No, no,' says Marcia, 'Carina's the girl. She looks like this.' She takes from a suitcase a gold statuette – could be a nymph. Caked in clay, like from a tomb: 'Hubert's not the father. How could I tell Carina that her father's dead? The bodyguard gone too.' she says.

In the case there's bracelets, nose jewels too. 'I keep a pawn activity,' says Marcia, 'just on the side. I stand a guy outside to buy the tickets when they leave. These never get redeemed.'

I think, 'So many things Nadia has never thought of.'

'You must think I'm a bad one, keeping everything locked away,' says Marcia: 'We'll go and find the guys that run the show. Where'd you suppose they'd be?'

'In the desert, in the mountains, with their guns. In narrow alleyways as well. The zealots, the ambitious. The dropouts, the flopouts. The desperate. Then there's some, the ones who've made it, sit on committees, make their choice. Then the bankers hop, and lots of guys get stuck into plastics in some factory,' I say.

Nadia asks, 'Did this Marcia put my cakes on show?'

'Of course,' I say. 'She's a rich one. Collects from graves, the poor. So, she needs servants. Like me. And we're to go and take vengeance on ...' I pause. Details don't come to mind.

'She's collected you. She's Fata Morgana,' says Nadia, starting to cry. 'You won't come back. There's no adventure if you don't survive, come back to exaggerate it all.'

Then there's Carina. More of Nadia's tears. She says,

'Gill died, of swelling. My, how you did bad to chivvy him. Peter's the visionary, sending the Fellows out, a cross nailed to each back.'

'Marcia's given me a job. I don't know what it is,' I say.

'Roots,' shouts Nadia. 'How I hate roots. That's what you'll look for. Bandits, priests and bankers. Oh, how I'd like to fly somewhere, another star, another planet, where they don't have roots, where they're just curious and never bored, and never do the same thing twice. And how I hate my fucking cakes, the twiddly message they send out – 'don't eat me or you'll break your jaw'. And jaw and jaw the people do, consume and spew it out, recycle, give a prize and write a little article, and snappers snap the useless stuff. Roots, roots – they're vegetables – long muddy straggly beardy drabs – they stare and stare at tiddly things. And then expound, romanticise, and cook the stuff as if it's happy pills ...' I turn away.

*

I tell Marcia – 'The potentates. I've made some lists, and put them into leagues. There's chiliasts, they've weaponry and say they know their stuff by heart. Then there's the guys who run their shows from offices and make you like what's in your past and maybe future too. But – Marcia, you shouldn't look at guys, and their philosophies: look at the structures, buried in the clays, the tiny skulls like mollusc shells that make a bed...'

'No, no, you silly boy,' she says: 'What d'you expect – you think we're off to tour around, and brave the pastors and imams, the suits, the uniforms? I know those guys – the different ways they want us all to live. Touring the living – that's no use. Remember – nothing is ever thrown away. That is why we collect, and why we can. Not everything nor everyone. Only survivors. But something's always there. A rusty patch – that's where an army drowned. That wicker cage – it's full of dodo shit, we can create a race of them anew... The same with guys: revelation, epiphany, abundance, parsimony. Let them fight it through again. No – I want to do exactly what I am! That is my vengeance.'

'Carina?' I ask: 'Where is she? Do we take her too?'

'We'll take her off her shelf, all in due course,' says Marcia, gathering speed. 'But first – it's mountains, deserts – that's where the bold men arise. The robbers, the austere, the kidnappers with one idea – down with the saints, the shrines, – bring order, levelling to the ground. Here comes equality, obedience, paths so straight the sheep won't stray, the goats all hurrying, racing to the muster. That's where regeneration comes – the Hyksos, throwing down the buildings, unhinging brightly-painted gates. Apocalyptic criminals! Tell Nadia,' Marcia shouts. 'They bring the concepts, then they start to cast them down. They are the harbingers of death. All is swept away – and then—'

'But Marcia—' I say.

On she races. 'Then they sow the seeds that sprout it up again. And I – collect the pieces. Sell them on. The crowds pour in to see the fruits of death. Those criminals inspired – onto the pyre, inventions, marketing, all crap – into the desert, out they drive the millions, into the waste, into oblivion ... but see! those empty mounds that were the capitals – they rise again. The hoardings, excavators ... Fucking architects. And off it goes again.' I say,

'So, Marcia – first it's murder, then it's death.'

'Of course,' she says. 'First massacres, then parliaments, then massacres again. First swords, then bombs. Look! what you call ideas – they're etched on those machete blades. Good harvests come from famines – surely you have noticed that?'

'It makes you sound like eating carrion,' I say.

'Of course. It's vital, that. Otherwise you'd see the evidences around, in stinking piles. I clear it all away and label it,' she says.

'It's horrible,' I say.

'You'd thought things otherwise,' says Marcia. 'That's quite natural. It isn't so, not like you thought.'

'It's your hypothesis,' I say.

She smiles. I say, 'Peter – sending bright guys out to run the world – it doesn't end so well.'

'Oh,' Marcia says. 'It depends where you are. It's order that's the goal, and also obstacle. You need it, but it isn't love – it's rather piles of skulls.'

'I don't believe in order, Marcia,' I say. 'Nadia does – creative steps along the railroad, joining all the compass points. But your collections – nothing's more orderly than that.'

'Ah yes,' she says. 'That isn't order, that is pattern, decoration. I had those comic books – a million of them. What does that imply? One issue every week. The weeks go by, you know, they add up into years. So what? Then, centuries. Not order, silly boy – that is duration. Then, there's replication, variations, serials, prayers on wheels, on flags. Routine, my dear.'

'What's to be done?' I ask.

'Did someone ask you what to do?' she laughs, 'Not all employers tell you what they think. Not like I've done. Imagine if you're working in a bank – what do your bosses consider their cosmology?'

'It's fine you tell me all this,' I say: 'I bet Carina goes still deeper.'

'What's all this about Carina?' Marcia says, angrily. 'You've got me before you, here – are you some bigot? Genetics – they obsess you? Just think, Barbarella's over seventy right now. You indefatigable Turks!'

Gill used to say, 'Statements you can't falsify are true.' True: that must be good, I guess, must stand for something. A real part of the big puzzle. So – I'm a Turkish athlete, with a stupid father, and I take after him.

Why not?

I say, 'I want my money, Marcia. I don't want yours.'

She says, 'I've given mine away – but it stays mine. The more you give away, the more the people think you've got lots more. Besides – they print it out in truckloads. Some you get to win on scratchcards – it can't be difficult to accumulate a pile.'

*

She takes us, Nadia and me, up to the roof. It's dark over the outside. We pass a guy, horizontal: 'He knows everything,' says Marcia, 'That's useful. I told you it was Sans Souci.'

'He's asleep,' says Nadia. 'Or dead.'

'Don't be so neurological,' Marcia says. 'He still knows everything.'

We look out over the expanse. There's towers: 'See,' Marcia says, 'they could be made of clay. Wind towers. Mosques, church spires, bells stirred by monks or air, or iron shards abandoned, tippitapping.'

'It's Radio City,' Nadia says.

'Of course it's radio,' Marcia says, barging along: 'Hear those deep registers – it's spaces underground that's cooling off. And there's a fire – the nomads make them when they sing ...'

'That could be Hoboken,' I say, though I've no idea.

'Yes,' says Marcia, 'of course, this could be modern city – those red lights up and down, like foxes' eyes. Or the walls could be of mud, grey green.'

'But if it isn't so,' says Nadia, 'it'll always be here, but suppose that isn't where you think it is? Then all other things can follow. Like – who's living here and strolling, who's in charge?'

'Exactly so,' says Marcia. 'You have grasped my point.'

This place – could be many places, could be nowhere – in the dark, it could be anywhere, except the restless cars... 'It's the capital,' I say, 'Of somewhere.'

'Goodness,' says Marcia, 'how ignorant you are. You're not at the centre any more. There's lots of centres. Arming what they said were good guys – now they turn out to be the worse. Well! That's proof, exactly what I say: those Americans – sowing dragons' teeth – and what comes up? Warriors, taking them from behind? Or dragons everywhere? When you don't win, you lose. It is the end. It's always happened so, you disappear. By marriages, if you're fortunate, a population transforms into another. Now, that's a truth.'

'That's your vendetta, then,' says Nadia, hammering in her nail. 'Marcia's on top, she hasn't had to stir. She sees the bad that's swept away, the worse arrives, and then becomes the bad.'

'Forget the goods and bads, Nadia. It's much more jumbled up. Retribution, borne by every sort of guy. What attracts me,' Marcia says, 'is the discarded stuff. It's there to go to auction. Make some fortunes. Wonderful! The portraits, and the rusted armour, mint sets of plastic Seven

Dwarfs. It all acquires a price, a certain rarity, a certain patina of worth, attraction, intrigue.'

*

Later, Nadia says to me, 'Marcia's all a contradiction.'

'No,' I say, 'it's us. We drift, we're blown along by Peter's handouts. That's our job. It brings the fear of death. The fear that we shall be cut off. The money ends. What next? The money, the award – it's our freedom and our dignity.'

'Well,' Nadia says, 'We're Marcia's now. I hope to do some stuff that ends in her collections – even if before too long it's thrown away.'

'The money's all the same,' I say, 'whether it's Peter's, or Marcia's. It all goes round and round. It all buys everything. Except your cakes, it seems. They have no market, Nadia. No stomach waits.'

'People want an orderly life,' says Marcia, 'and so do I. But what a price! It's terrible, that order. Only – its shards seem to be collectable.'

*

Peter dresses all in white, with espadrilles. Like a colonial. Like a Colombian, as if those towers are Bogotà. As if outside there's real people – in the gym, in the street, selling chickens and leeks, dancing and telling lies. While he carries on – guiding the Fellows. Plotting the new buildings, the treaties. Gill favoured corduroy.

Between me and Nadia, there's sometimes friction, like in a movie, not amounting, a tension without too many sounds – 'Something by Supervielle,' says Nadia. 'Like the string of an oud,' she says.

We're traitors to Peter, now we're with Marcia, though it's not clear what that will mean. Marcia favours flowers, her clothes are full of them. Also butterflies. I think Carina was invented – maybe it was her, Marcia, when young. Hubert is mostly quiet, hiding in his wall. I'm convinced there's no Carina. Just an obstacle, a fantasy. You can be punished, maybe, if you raise, then kill, one of those fantastic animals, or people fantasised. Too bad – I could have lost my head for someone like Carina.

'You remind me of someone,' Nadia says.

'That's good,' I say.

Athletic. Ridiculous. A critic.

*

Peter says, 'You two will pass to the other side, I know. Marcia's. Unreason. The unambitious. No trumpets will sound for you. The scandal of Gill's death ... just as well to keep it quiet. My foundation – when you produce the bosses of the world, some will cut their corners. Gill hoped they'd all come back. I'm pleased they won't. Some will be real bad, no doubt, but sometimes that is better so. It's in their genes. You—' he turns to me, 'You could be a critic, yes. The murder's in your blood. Your father's blood. Or you could turn out nothing, worthy of respect, like all the no ones, nameless narrators of the woolly script – but null. Nadia .. If you're Salomé, do you sing as well as dance? You must do both, if you're to get the severed head.'

He waves us away.

'Now, Peter's the captain of his pirate ship,' says Marcia. 'You did a good turn to kill his mate. Both he and Gill, they saw you as a hitman – firing you up, an angry man, no talents in a lofty place. But – you got Gill. He hadn't time to bargain.'

'I was set up do some rough deed?' I ask. 'But not that lucky accident?'

'A hitman, to take out individuals – that is always useful,' Marcia says. 'The big guys – don't do anything themselves. You losers – that is what you're for. The little things that hurt the soul of people at the top, resentments, rivalries, people who cross them ... you're there to take them out.'

'Nadia, then – maybe for her they had in mind some Holofernes – some guy, some sex, and then the tent peg through his eye? Having her cake, and then ...' I say, not believing.

'Well, there's been stranger things,' says Marcia: 'Consider Scylla – turned into a zoo of horrid animals, monstrous dogs, and all those heads! For what enlightenment would call a peccadillo ...'

*

I tell Nadia, I regress; if she takes this, she will take anything:

'I'm a child. They won't let me have animals. Maybe the neighbours shoot them. But – "No, we don't want you anthropomorphising sentiments. A beast's a beast. Not one of us. Here's the book that tells it so."

'I'm not so sure. I lie in bed, and think. Parents – what are they, what are they supposed to do? If I run and twist, I'll grow so I don't need them. Bringing food to me. If I don't eat, maybe they'll go away. Nothing personal, they're just closed up in another room – their parents killed, maybe, in quite some other place. Tall anxious birds, disgorging unspeakable stuff, thrusting it down my throat. Did they misread the book, and so attract its curse? Squawking beasts.'

'Don't do psychology on me,' says Nadia: 'You can be happy and be angry too. Carina's not your sister, long-lost or stolen. She doesn't exist. I know you must have had parents – you were lucky to have two of them. Think if you had come out of an egg!'

'You idiots!' says Marcia. 'Until history hits you, it's all trivial, to pass the time. Then – you lose your money, or your life, usually it's over quick, if the paperwork is sorted out. The rest, what comes before, is playing in the street or reading dirty books. If big events assail you, it's for a reason you had not imagined, or for none at all. Things aren't linked up, you mustn't think they are.'

Nadia wears her artist's clothes. Black or white, they're nothing much, smelling of her own old sweat, that's what you remember most about her, binds you tight.

'The trouble is,' says Marcia, 'you two, you're both last century, or even more. For you, it's either-or. Forget it. Just say what you think, don't think of some riposte, some other world hypothesised, starting with a doubt – your "either", then some quite other thing you haven't even thought about, the "or". That way – you're stuck. No wonder guys with guns will kill your geese, your cat, and then go after you. You're nailed down on the threshhold, asking for some monstrous thing you knew would come. Some time – either now, or later.'

'He's like that,' says Nadia. 'That's not me. He has a past, he's made it up. I haven't got a thing, and it is better so.'

'Well,' says Marcia, 'however it turns out, don't expect help from me. Look what I've got.' She inflates, unfolds, a room. It's a *singerie*: 'Someone didn't need it,' says Marcia. The monkeys mostly glare. Some are interested in tuning their instruments, some in combing wigs. Others strut, orate. 'Is that a bomb they're making?' I ask. 'No, it's a round pudding,' Marcia says, 'Ask Nadia. And don't be so fearful. It's only a metaphor.'

'You should stop accumulating,' Nadia says. 'Start buying my stuff.'

'I told you,' Marcia says. 'It shouldn't need a *singerie* to show you. You must make your world, and get out of Peter's. It's quite unavailing, him sending out those

Fellows. They're bottles in a sea of bottles, each with a message. They're bound to end up like these monkeys, these little devils,' she says, testing the fixity of the paint with her long thumb. 'I'm your lighthouse,' she says, 'But those rocks move around.'

I say to Nadia, 'It all sounds portentous, but I don't know what we're supposed to do.'

'I know,' says Nadia. 'That's why I'm a creative and you're a scholar. Of sorts.'

'Marcia loves people seeming to do things, knowing that's only the half of it,' I say. 'Being a monkey usually takes up your time.'

'Be off with you!' Marcia says, and laughs: 'What's the best thing for you, Nadia?'

'Kissing in the cinema.' she says promptly. 'Saying I'm in love. Things like that.'

'Well, I guess you're hetero, Nadia,' Marcia says.

'Yes, that's just the half of it,' Nadia says, and laughs.

I say, 'Peter always told us – never hurt an individual, but get used to thinking of a mass of them. Suffering is part of everything. Think of the future generations, think of your destiny ...'

'Yes,' says Marcia, 'that's most interesting. Those generations, kind of Faustian, stretching out in front as well as back, and yet determining. Where are they? What do they want? Spit on our bones, you bet.'

'Those Fellows,' Nadia says. 'The leaders, wise guys of all sorts – they didn't have to learn those books by heart, not like I did.'

'You didn't learn all those?' I ask, amazed. 'There's no room in your head for other things.'

'Oh,' Nadia says, 'it fades, like wallpaper. I guess you slackers said you'd learnt, and didn't.'

Marcia laughs, 'The wallpaper! Nadia, you're quite baroque. Putting paper on the walls! So bookish!'

'I know it all,' says Nadia: 'What's in the books, the canvas round the walls, the hum and drum of music as you eat world food. And then? What do you do with all of it? It's gourmet fare, and once inside, it merely stops you dying premature.'

Marcia says, 'Well, Nadia, there's your aesthetic – a fine idea, churned round, left as a tiny coil of waste amid the sand.'

Nadia smiles. She always does. 'Peter reminds me of a Mickey Mouse,' she says, 'who's started off the wizard's brooms. Disaster they'll bring, and sorcerers don't return to sort it out.'

Marcia says, 'Gill instead, loved going native. Everywhere. He took the strangeness in his stride – he loved that beetle stew, danced naked in the fire. And how they laughed at him, the natives, everywhere, and piled it on.'

'I had a dream,' I say. 'In Mexico, a bar – you asked for rum or cognac, whisky or a gin, and always "no!" You never found out what they really had. We ran and ran, on to the next – an accident, maybe, my companion, then streets of magenta houses, low and quiet ... Then there's a guy, comes up and tells my girl, it seems she's hurt –

"When you're dead, you'll have my face." And so it seems
– his face identical to hers, and so the dead exchange their
features with the newly or the nearly dead, and on it
goes...'

'You'll not have my face, never,' Marcia says.

'Perhaps I'll have yours,' Nadia says to me, 'Round
and round they go. Like money – that has faces on it too.
Nothing makes the world go round like death.'

'Now,' says Marcia, captivated by the doings in her
singerie, 'That "round and round"'s a thing I never
believed. It's quite against nature, seeing all the effort
people put in staying still, accumulating.'

'Marcia, you accumulate like the sorcerers and
witches do,' says Nadia. 'Spells and brooms.'

I wonder what Nadia takes. I – we're – not supposed
to use the substances. I guess she goes out clubbing, not
taking me, doing her head-splits and her tiny crying – a
world unknown, I'm sure, to Peter, as to me. The only time
I believe in God is when they ask me to do drugs. Gill
wasn't modern, but he took everything he could, they say.

'Being modern means playing with your shape, your
face,' says Marcia, meditating: 'Maybe it's right, but I
prefer external things to touch – chalcedony, papyrus,
moleskin, shagreen, walrus ivory. Those flutes too –
they'd bring the spirit from you, if I'd let you play!'

'Hey, guys!' I say. 'We're into world schemes, not
shifting our own ganglia,' and Marcia says 'How Turkish!'

'We're to go and find stuff for Marcia,' Nadia says,
'Then she'll cosset it, give it away, and be richer. In the

spirit too.'

Wherever we go, there's danger,' I say.'I expect it's animals she's after. Invented ones. We have to watch for Peter's emissaries.'

'More Alice!' Nadia says. That's for me. Landscapes with moving figures!'

'You can take anything you want,' says Marcia. 'Take it with you, multiply, and bring it back. It ought to be a sequence, a coherent category, that is all. Nadia picks; you – you're just the shotgun.'

'Anything he wants,' says Nadia, pointing to me. 'So long as he stops dwelling on the past, especially his. It's seen as affectation, that brooding. It all derives from provocation – Peter and Gill, making it up for him, our fearsome history.'

'Peter and his luncheons,' Marcia says, 'may have an impact where you go. How they work it goes like this – cash for some cultural exchange. Then seminars to sow the seed. Then experts go out, map the scene. They lay a base, far off, some country hitherto unknown, preparing it to get our military, our diplomats. A crisis over there – and we, and all our friends, are all in place, the other guys are "on the spot".'

Nadia says, 'Marcia, it is always so, the way it's done is this!'

We're two who can't be shocked, or so we think, Nadia and I. Then Marcia says, 'There is a little thing I'd ask you to seek out, bring back. It's rather – specialised ... even a transgressive kind of stuff.'

'Not shrunken heads?' asks Nadia.

'No, no,' says Marcia, 'they're gruesome. No – you're only partly right. I'm after shrunkens – heads still attached, and all the rest.'

She takes down shoeboxes. Inside, there's little cadavers – some white, some black, some like sea cucumbers, some soapstone, some alabaster, and some indigo.

'Who are they?' Nadia asks.

'Oh, mostly philosophers,' Marcia says, 'Some generals, and other high-up guys. I told you – here's Sans Souci. This is where they have their home. They make no sound, no smell ...' she goes on, opening the little boxes, spilling out some dwarflets, others, she cradles them, stroking them like kittens.

'Hubert began all this,' she says. 'But now he's lost the taste. He fears them – thinks how he'll end up as one of them ... No chance! No hope! He's not their caliber.'

'To me, it's all quite normal,' Nadia says. 'Even too much so.'

'Of course,' says Marcia. 'There's books and paintings to collect but – in those, there can be anything: false, perverse – realities you wouldn't wish to see. Not mentioning the sights unreal.'

'You're right, Marcia,' says Nadia, 'but you could collect those just the same.'

Marcia takes a mannikin, holds it to the light: 'It's like translucent jade,' she says. 'More natural than this – you could not find. Behind it – there are hunters, then emblamers, all with their skills arcane ...'

'Aha!' I say. 'There's hunters. So, these guys fell in the chase.'

'Just some of them,' Marcia says vaguely. 'Don't let it worry you. This is refinement, nothing brutal, nor premature. It's art and history combined. Remember – everything ends up everywhere.'

'I thought this had been stopped, this trade,' I say.

'Oh well, they've stopped so many things,' says Marcia. 'They can't stop the shrunks, however hard they try ... It's profit, people come to see the stuff when I am tired of it. All down to size, and beautiful. They look like aliens, don't you think? Maybe that's what we are, puffed up, then tiny in our box.'

'We'll go where there's casualties,' Nadia says: 'The idea attracts. Who wants tapestries when the hunt's outside? We need women in there too, I guess.'

'That's the spirit!' Marcia shouts. 'Peter will plot, and build museums – but you'll take the philosophers, and they'll live in miniature for ever ... well, "live" it's maybe not.'

Nadia's keen: Marcia says, 'Nominalists are the easiest, but idealists – the light shines through! They're precious rocks. You'll find the legal bunch – more like sea worms, a-wriggle. Positivists – logical or not – you shouldn't worry about the reputation, that they're rather crass. In the end, they come out various, orange-ribbed or violet. The generals too – some yellow as chanterelles, soft as cèpes, others – puffballs. I have room for all of them.'

They chatter on.

I feel awkward. Maybe this non-life after non-death, miniaturised, is what the holy books have glimpsed. Stuck in a case, forever. Everyone knowing what you said, and you can't change a word. Myself, I'd sooner hell was portering – maybe carting harps, and being shouted at. I try to feel some warm thought. Can I regret Gill, feel the pain, that I had caused an accident ... Some contradiction there, the 'causing accidents'? I wish it had been Peter, and not Gill. I wish it had been both of them.

'I'm so fond of you two,' Marcia says. 'Really, I love you.'

'That's cute,' says Nadia. 'I guess those little dead guys – makes the prospect seem quite dwindled, when it comes to you yourself. Just small and dumb, you end. It's neat, it says it all. Genealogy, affect ... all in a jar. A box for shoes. Yes, you've caught on to something there. Those old cabinets, the ancestors, the blobs of jewels – the skill – a waste! A waste to make, a waste to see. While you're sidling up those aisles to see old stuff – you could be watching frogs on kingcups: anything would do.'

Marcia doesn't take it in: she says, 'You take what Peter does so seriously! Americans, their warriors and their wars! The mess! It makes you feel quite tenderly. On the up, there's guys much smarter, take the plots quite seriously, not thinking of the dog and playing shuffleboard back home. Guys who really know what empire and the warring states can be, and why it matters to them, number one priority. Poor Peter ... when it doesn't make me sad, it makes me laugh.'

'It's not the project, Marcia, it's the person,' Nadia says, 'Needs taking down.'

'Well, ruling the world attracts, I guess,' says Marcia, not much caring. 'Even the Turks have had a try,' and she pinches me.

'I'm not—' I start.

'You must be something, dear,' says Marcia. 'We must label you.'

'—an athlete,' I go on, 'but I can wrestle.'

'That you'll need,' says Marcia. 'Tickle, if you cannot grasp,' and Nadia looks with new respect, at both of us.

*

'I long to hunt for shrunks,' says Nadia, later. 'I love the chase. Most things are stuck down, passive, hung on walls, in houses, quite unmoving. Sometimes switched on, but mostly not. My aim is not like Marcia's, though.'

'But – cakes, dear Nadia,' I say. 'It's naff. I won't say twee.'

'You haven't understood a thing,' she says. 'You eat them, and they churn to crap. If they're enamelled, you'll just starve to death.'

'That's true!' I say. 'That's admirable. I hadn't thought.'

'Marcia collects her stuff,' Nadia goes on, 'because it's a detritus. Everything that's ended up as junk, or just by being old and framed – it's not eternal. That might be its last hope. It's junk. It may be pretty, but its value's found only when you pay in cash at auction. The money must be fresh. And what you buy – is not.'

'The junk is destined to become junk,' I puzzle through – and reach the truth, 'and even disappear.'

'Fuck!' I say aloud, 'That is banal.'

'And true,' says Nadia. 'But don't think you're among the first to get to it. For Marcia, it is politics, humanity as well.'

*

'Those guys at lunch,' says Marcia, 'they're plotting what comes next. Peter's afraid of them – he thinks because they've got religion, and since he believes only in himself, they're a better lot than him. It's an illusion. They are seeds, that's waiting for the wind to scatter, everywhere. Now, take my shrunks – I don't despise the bad guys that's among them. Good and bad, they're just reduced, collectable. It's me they give their pleasure to. There is no pain for me. I do not judge. I just amass.'

'Beyond the good guys, and the bad ...' says Nadia. 'It seems to me that it's an illusion too. Being immortal, Marcia, doesn't change a thing. The cards, the dice, are still the same, however many years you've put behind. You're not detached, however long you last – the game remains. The words – the good, the bad – their meanings change, and on you play. You seek, you stare...'

'Yes, Nadia,' says Marcia impatiently. 'You stare,

you seek – but what? For your satisfaction, it may be good to understand the things to do, and not. But – it's all anomalies. It's bad to kill your enemy – but it depends .... at times, it seems the normal thing to do, the good. It's context, Nadia. What I do, is find a context where it all suspends. The shrunks are there, in silence, shrunken, tiny. You wonder – what did you people do, before? If I were interested, how might I judge? Peter collects like me, except his guys can stand and leave, quite educated, knowing stuff by heart.'

'Yes, yes,' I say. 'Of course it's difficult – but we shall answer nothing here. And you don't mean anomaly, you mean anachronism – and that gets nowhere. It's like laughter, you laugh at the incongruous, but that can't tell you much. First, you must establish what is congruous – then, the exceptions tickle you.'

'Apes laugh,' says Nadia. 'And we're incongruous. Come on, let's hunt the shrunks.'

'People despair of nature,' I say. 'So they invent these animals, the fantasies, who come to help you out. Maybe...'

'No,' says Nadia. 'Forget your curious beasts. No animals, only bodikins.'

'Try Mongolia,' shouts Marcia, as we leave. 'China is out, and India's unlikely too. Try steppes – even giant ones.'

'I want that bird that's a hundred, a thousand other birds,' I tell Nadia.

'All birds are that. All things are. Why multiply?' she

asks. 'That's just more naff. If you go in for beauty – you can't have two things – two the same, or different. That blows the idea apart. Of course, things blown apart may be your passion.'

'Just want to hold it in my arms, and see its yellow eye,' I say.

'Tiny things,' shouts Marcia after us, 'Those too. Take an egg to pack them in. Books within books, things too large to move. Lost cities. Peoples absorbed. Large structures underground. I know they all exist, and I'll collect them all.'

Nadia grumbles. 'The packing may take all our lives,' she says. 'Marcia should wait till they all come up in auctions. We'll need to deal with Peter's emissaries – the guys who're ministers. Smiles, greed, and family – that is them. Then, there's a few that's brigands – they're the chancers who hold on to marvellous things, or else they burn them. All Peter's graduates. Marcia's a humanist, that's for sure – making sure it's us that takes the risks.'

We set off.

Peter sends people out, Marcia sucks them back, reduced. Where is our place in this? Is this my quest?

'Hey,' I shout, 'Marcia! She didn't give us any money, Nadia!'

'Your animals, her relics – I don't think they come through cash,' she says.

Interiors

Dr Osman says, 'There's interiors you can decorate, and interiors you must try to empty.' He's one of Peter's graduates. He keeps a table, a high table, with dignitaries around. Scientists, archaeologists – measurers, diggers, zoomen. There's a guy who snorkels, looks like Aurel Stein, the cave explorer. Fish men, bird men, a lady with a hat the little boys wear for circumcisions. It's quite a college. In comes a dish, and all reach out their hands. The talk is technical, of kills and syllables, extinctions, disappearing rites.

Osman says, shouting above the babble, and the scraping of the communal plate – 'Here is my family.' Around the walls they stand in frames – pictures in inks on isinglass, it seems, the faces with a slight surprise, like funerary Copts. 'You see,' says Osman, 'The family eyebrow.' The relatives all look the same, world-weary, quizzing. The current family eats beside – a slit of antechamber, silently, the women serve. They giggle when we slide our faces in.

'Peter said, to bring the whiteys in. Not put like that, perhaps, but there they are. My Fellows,' Osman says: 'I should have liked a humanist or two, but there they are, my cutting edge. Now – interiors ... I've filled the palace up with *trompe l'œil*. It's painted like a cave, you see beyond the demigods and holy men some scenes of Deauville, bathers. Races too.' There it is, Kentucky Derby, and landscapes of flesh, inflated, tiny feet and rubber balls. He holds us close, I see his hand is steering Nadia's rump. He says,

'This here's the interior you must fill. Then there's your own, that you must empty. And then you wait. What comes?' he chuckles. 'A robin, perhaps? A lark? Wait, and then wait, prepare the space. Don't twirl, and don't intone ... Wait – and you'll see, there's nothing come that isn't there already. An interior. What more could you want?' He glares, as we think of answers. He grips my arm: 'That's it. Interior. Do you grasp? It is what it is – a rare moment, even rarified.'

Two guys are playing *tars* – almost inaudible: 'That's the effect!' says Osman, 'You don't notice, then you do, and then you listen. The music that there's been is gone for good, and what comes out, it wisps away like smoke.'

Nadia whispers, 'We can't ask him about antiquities. Nor what is new.'

Osman goes on, 'The technique lies over there,' and he waves to the West: 'The spirit's here. These guys,' and he waves at the high table, its celadon, its plastic beakers, 'May save a fish, a toad, a snail. What satisfaction does that give to you, to me? Maybe some guys will come to see – I ask again, what satisfaction does that give, to me, to you?'

I am a critic, but I don't say that – it is a trade ambiguous, and might even be – it doesn't quite exist... Maybe the critics go to jail, where there's no *trompe l'œil*.

'More paintings, and more emptiness. Feel how tense it gets! Preserve things as they were, while we float on, ephemeral as clouds, our hands reach out, and wisps and sticks is all we find. Those snails and flies my Fellows save – their habitat renewed and stocked – while we grow thin and jaded,' Osman says, sadness over his round face, waning like a moon, and over ours as well, 'Shrink and wrinkle, dry and crack: farewell our bodies ... our ears are full of ancient sounds, we cannot hear the music, in our heads a bell is sounding, you can't switch it off. It's an electric one,' he says, and laughs, mocking, probably himself. 'Eternal life! The frogs, the beetles ... on and on. That's what these guys give – a promise of eternity to all who hop and creep. And us? We shrink away, we fear the future and the past.'

'It's true, how true,' says Nadia, weeping: 'It all turns into crap, even the parasites within. Only the flies grow plump.'

We meditate. His hands are everywhere, Nadia must be sensing them, they follow every billow of her, every sounding cave, and every teat.

The Fellows finish off, congratulate each other on the fluid talk they've had.

'Now we play football,' says the snorkeller: 'Come, you, and join the game!' he shouts to me.

'No, no, I am no athlete,' I shout back. I feel at one with Nadia. Will she drop into this stereotype's embrace?

Later, Nadia says, 'Well! That was refreshing. As I suspected, one way or another, all Peter's graduates are missionaries.'

'I felt I had a duty to you, Nadia,' I say, 'But Osman

seems a rich and powerful man, not to be crossed.'

'Almost everything is experience,' Nadia says, 'And you could have been playing football.'

'The experts and the profs – they're biologists and physicists. They'd have laughed at my thin legs,' I say.

'They play with a rag ball, a Turk's head,' she says: 'And now we eat. Goat! I love it. That round table – lunch, and goat, is served all day, you just move round, there's plastic stuff you don't need wash.'

'Maybe there's philosophers among those guys,' I say, 'that could be shrunk.'

'No, no,' she says, 'Osman's is the vision. All the fellows here are into culture, rites, and particles: the bigger picture – that is on the walls. You know, they sell this sand, it goes to beaches everywhere – to Deauville too, I'd bet. That's what I call spreading an idea. You lie on it, and turn quite brown; or black, if you're already brown.'

'Frivolity,' I say. 'Nadia, we have a duty to pursue.'

'I love your feeling dutiful about me,' Nadia says. 'It means I don't need watch the things I do.'

'It's Peter,' I say. 'His plan means paying guys who're meritorious to be more so. It's sharpening their values, or giving some, if they are short. Then, when the guys are done, Marcia coddles them, and puts them in her store.'

'A power of synthesis you surely have,' says Nadia. 'But that leaves things out. The skin on skin. The chatter in high rooms.'

'The drawing on the walls ..' I say, 'I'm leaving out

the dark, the poisonous.'

We eat. Osman and Nadia do what they must do, what comes most natural. Without their clothes. I say, 'We should take something. Remember our bargain with Marcia, our word.'

'Oh,' she says, 'what fun! So, you're a thief! Osman only gives – I certainly shan't take.'

'I'll take his eye,' I say. 'The one that's not deceived. The one that watches everything – the jails, the kitchens, and the family: the bank, the market, and the wire.'

'It's just a metaphor,' she says. '"The eye deceived"– it really isn't so. You know it, but you pretend it isn't so.'

'Nadia,' I say, 'I'm not a democrat. I'll cause some suffering if it serves. I flunked from Peter's course, remember. Now – did you bring that egg, like Marcia said? You didn't put it in your cakes?'

She laughs – 'Marcia was right, you are a cheeky boy! Now, take the eye, I'll put it in the shell. The yolk will keep it moist.'

The eye is high up, on the wall – the middle eye, some figure done in abalone shell. I guess from there you see the city and the steppe, inside the jails, the schools and everywhere, and Peter's textbooks, plans for digging here and there, and buying motorcars, and driving up and down in them, past shops.

'Just like a Turk,' laughs Nadia. 'You fogey! All this stuff is frippery. The eye – you're right. That is what counts. Keeping a watch on everything. You thief! I doubt that it will work when we have gouged it out.'

'Give me a hand,' I say. 'These middle eyes – require a great physique to gouge them out. It doesn't matter if they never work – you need the family, the wealth, the panorama: only those can power your sight.'

'Stealing!' Nadia says, 'it primes you!'

'He stole it from a cave,' I say, 'Dunhuang, maybe. And Marcia stole the egg from – who knows, a fabulous bird. Its yolk – that must be worth a lot. The eye, the pearl ... and the idea. Where did the idea come from? Meditation. Emptiness. Interiors. For after all, there's nothing in your eye, but everything has passed before, the tricks it learns are good for everywhere, including dark and fabulous things,' and on I go, and Nadia says, 'There is still room inside the shell for cities lost and buried. Although they certainly exist it's hard to find a place for them within this narrow space.'

'Forget it, Nadia – we have started well. This eye is rare – you don't want unique things, or else it seems they've thrown the other similars away, as being worthless or too common to collect,' I say. I'm keen to leave before there's trouble and the table fills with guys for tea ...

'Osman gives them five meals a day, like they were used to,' Nadia says. It must have been a confidence she got from him, a warm moment: 'It doesn't leave much room for football.'

I say, 'Those guys – they're looking on the ground for bugs or at things invisible in the sky – they don't see what's in between.'

'It's Osman's job,' says Nadia. 'Keeping order. A

regime for everyone.'

Peter's out of date – we have this list of guys, his graduates, to visit – but it's not about his country being top, nor about some other. Everything is everywhere, guys invent themselves wherever they are found, they all come out quite like. Their problems are the same, besides, Peter's into facing down, not solving anything.

'Osman's not a throwback, he's like all the rest,' I say.

'That's good!' says Nadia, 'And he doesn't try to solve a thing – he's not obsessive. But for sure, there'll be some place where you can be anything at all, and no one notices or cares.'

'Maybe Japan,' I say: 'That city where there's everyone. They all wear uniform, and there's no army. But, Nadia – yours is the international style. You're everywhere at home, and everywhere cast out.'

'That is your commonplace,' she says. 'Look where we are – this desert looks like Atacama. Waterless. These guys must leave, forget their songs and dances.'

It's true. We two – we've already left, the songs forgotten; we don't dance.

Perhaps I'll find a cave that's filled with stoppered jars and birchbark scrolls. Make sense of all the animals, the hybrids, blessed and cursed by spirits, jumbled up.

There's a guy, he strums an instrument: there's four strings, it's short in the body, long neck ending in a horse's head. He says, 'You cosmopolitans! afraid you've lost something on your path – it's useless looking for philosophers. The big picture – it's a poster on the wall, and everyone's familiar with it. You must realise – you're looking for some stuff to sell, to take back somewhere rich, and that is all.'

'Quick!' says Nadia. 'Make him an offer for that thing. I'm certain Marcia doesn't have one ...' and I do. 'I bet he sells a lot of them,' she says.

It won't fit in the egg, of course, and so we dump it when we're out of sight.

'You should consider this,' says Nadia. 'People joined with animals. It's not about nature, it's about us. Minotaurs.'

She's right. 'Nadia,' I say, 'Do you have an unexamined life?'

'I try,' she says. 'Not to pry in it. It's early days. Putting your thoughts in artefacts – it lets you off examinations.'

It means I must examine mine. Then – 'No, Nadia – we can't carry those!' I shout. We have no cash – she's buying canvases.

'Don't fuss!' she shouts. 'You try to put a shaping to it all, your life. You waste your time – your life is not a script. The only voice is yours. Who cares who likes or hates you – all the pain that comes from doing down your enemies ...' She is still shouting when some guys – they must be auctioneers or painters – carry her off. I see her legs kick out.

A painting's left behind – enormous, bigger than the real, of how the scene should be, the planes as sharp as claws, the rocks piled into shaky drifts.

'Look, look,' shouts Nadia, 'no people. That's how it should be. Look what they're doing to me ..' and they drag her off, to ransom for no cash, to violate – no joy for anyone.

'Stand firm, Nadia,' I shout back. 'They're not Mongolians, those always laugh, they are tattooed. These guys are from another world ...' Maybe the secret of her work, her artistry, is seeking for this other world of strangers. International style. There are no hands, no eyes. She keeps them for herself.

The painting, hard edge – it has its flowers already fixed. Behind, in the Mongolian grass, the red, the blue, the flowers, the ferny plants – wild roses and – there goes a hare almost too fast to see ...

I have a duty to her. I rest beneath a low tree. There's someone on the other side – I say, 'Mongolia doesn't look like I remember,' and I peer at the picture.

The guy, Togon's his name, says, 'Nothing is quite like – the painting, what it was, what it is.'

That's folksy, but I ask, 'You Mongolians – now, you've no generals, and never had philosophers. We're working for a friend, who looks for shrivelled things. Like large silkworms. Maybe ... Or animals, invented. Needed for a book. With pictures too,' I say.

'Animals like that are quite incongruous,' he says. 'That's what they're for. Life here is dull, although we don't get bored. But – this friend – what do you get for searching, what's the prize?'

'Nothing, I guess,' I say, noting for the first time that the truth's appeared, and stands between us.

He smiles a disappearing smile. 'The time goes quicker here,' he says, 'than once before. Look how the landscape shifts – they dig, they build, they flood. No time for animals. Not much for painting flowers.'

*

Here's Nadia! Bruised, but otherwise ...

'They dropped me,' Nadia says. 'Besides, I knew that you would come and rescue me. Those guys – they didn't see the joke. It was a pricing question, now resolved.'

'Your friends seem much like enemies,' says Togon. 'Those here, those there. They want to rule the world – or else stack up mementoes come from everywhere. Archive, or booty? You must ask yourselves. These silent desiccated heroes that you seek – are they trophies – or the record?'

I don't know,' says Nadia, 'and I don't care. They're like the votary samples people leave – the stillborns and the arms, the legs, the proof that some religion and its demigods has worked. You just say "thanks" – no one responds. Never. Never, never. They send you out, they kidnap you, they take your house, your virtue if you think it's yours... You travel light. The world won't end, empires go on and leave their prints – and if instead it disappears, all, everywhere – you've not been taken in. You paint your scene, put your enamels in the fire. You change your shape, you move where you've been told. And in the end – promotion! Or, it may be – execution! Oblivion! All three! Who knows, and who foretells?'

'We're lost, here in Mongolia. Doubting the motives of our sponsor,' I say despairing.

'I don't want certainties, I want adventures,' Nadia says. 'The last one didn't hurt a bit. Not much. Those guys – they fix the prices. That way, a country knows it's doing well or bad. Some countries do so bad, you feel they must rise up. It isn't so, but that way we all hope and theorise.'

Togon says, 'If it's culture you're after – Mongolia's full of those invented animals. When the road came through here, there were those giant silkworms, like big caterpillars. You guys have the phoenix – that's your dream. We have spirits – or we had them. We were the warriors then,' and he emotes, grows tearful, 'Our horses...'

'Quiet!' I shout. 'Forget the fantasies. I just invented those to keep that Peter quiet – then there was death, and Gill was gone. Playing those games with me – it had to stop ... Besides – the Road, the Silk Road – it never passed through here.'

'Muddling up the categories,' Nadia says, 'fiddling with nature and the laws of gravity – it is a fateful thing, it marks the end. There's nowhere else to go, imagination runs its course, and drops and fades and dies.'

I think Nadia's beating did her damage. We can't travel on like this, meeting people. What life would that be?

I say, 'Lying – I do it, when it helps, but I can't stand other people doing it to me.'

Nadia says, 'Yes! That's talking.'

She's regressed, it seems to me. Maybe they battered her about the head, took off the adult self.

'Togon,' I say, 'you're not the kind of Buddhist Gill was after. You'd not qualify for Peter's fellowships. Tell us more about this place, no fancy tales!'

'It's spirits that have an animal form,' he says, 'Some are black Then, there's one called Yāma, fierce and blue. A bull's head, a necklace made of skulls. You know, we have a card game too, over a hundred types of animal! Thirty kinds of rabbit!'

'Mongolians wrestle, like the Turks,' says Nadia: 'I think they are the Turks that stayed behind.'

'I'm not involved,' I say. 'My body shape informs you so.'

He shows us his apartment. I say to Nadia, 'I feel uncomfortable, when this is done to me. People who ask you in.'

There's a line of teapots, red, with swirls. A bright blue plastic bowl. I can't praise one without the other, so I leave both out, unsaid.

'Don't worry about me,' Nadia says. 'I don't. I could stay here, branch out, paint the spirits.'

'We don't do that now so much,' says Togon. Suddenly, he wants us both to go. Outside, we hear the chatter, many feet. 'My father was a general,' he says.

Maybe they tried to shrink him. There's a closet. He

could be in there, his uniform at least.

It's like Togon was a sleeper, Peter's sleeper. Ready for campaigns deep in the future. Nadia says to me – 'I feel good. I wear my black pants, white top. Black top, white pants – not good.'

I say, 'It's sweet you dress for me.'

'Oh no,' she says. 'For me. For you, I'd put on – cerise and arsenic.'

'That's good too, Nadia,' I say. 'That's bold. And – you have all the odd adventures ...'

'Being beaten's not so good. You'd like it too?' she asks: 'That Yāma – I guess I saw a bit of him. A paw, up from where he frowsts.'

I think – there must be something, something about behaving naturally, that drives them all, Mongolians, and Peter's guys. I say, 'Why shouldn't Gill and Peter want to send their guys around the world? There's others do it. Few who don't.'

'It's not natural for them,' Nadia says. 'It's hubris. And around their necks, they've skulls.'

We leave Togon – but at his door, he tries to show us photos – 'This is how it was,' he says.

'No, no,' says Nadia. 'Like everyone, we've seen them, photos. They don't tell a tale.'

We scamper down the stairs. There's crowds there, whispering. They wait to see Togon. Maybe he sorts their problems out, gives them a name, at least. A great man, a shaman, after all.

A guy who lives below pops out and says, 'Hey, are

you two *pédés* too? You didn't see his pics? Maybe you'd like a game of chess – here, we all play. We invented chess.'

We don't have the brains for chess. Is it a shrine here? Maybe a cinema? Pleasure palace?

We go outside. There's water on the ground, quite deep. It wasn't here before.

I say, 'I guess these guys could grow some things, if they had the mind. But – we're in trouble. We've only got that eye; it doesn't fill the egg, it's blind, and everyone, if they collect or not, has got an eye, or two.'

It is a moment quite disconsolate. 'The track ends here,' says Nadia.

Then we see – a sign, stuck in the wet: 'Dig Here,' it says.

*

'I know it's stones,' the foreman says, as we dig down, our wetsuits clag – Nadia takes hers off in front of us, puts on a tiny suit. 'We don't know what the stones are for, but surely, they must have a use.' Some are painted, some are cut. The painted ones lie out along the path – 'jewel in the lotus', they spell out. Over and over. We are satisfied. They have a use.

'Now,' says the foreman, 'you obedient pair, seeking your treasures – down you go. Swim down. There is a team that comes from far away, to see if guys like you can get accustomed to the element. Grow gills.'

'Oh no,' I think, 'it's Peter's experts from Beijing this time, and murder comes to haunt. Now there's a plethora of gills awaiting ...' Maybe it's nemesis, my murder trial begins ... Gill ...! And with glee, Nadia takes off her costume, black and white in lozenges – she shouts, as she dives down, 'I could live down here for ever, here's the spirits ...' and there are! Fish, of every kind and none. The foreman says, 'By night, you'll help in the mess hall, where the truckers eat. It should be simple – they're from everywhere, and taste and dietary rules proliferate. It should be easy – fish and such are scale or skin or shell. But no one knows which one is which – you must select and kill and cook. There's slow cook, and there's fast. Nadia will do the quick, and you the slow.'

'What fun!' shouts Nadia. 'Enough of those antiques! Collecting stuff macabre and drear. And experts coming – maybe they won't play soccer, but creative games – it could be softball, or it might be chess. For certain we can play it in the water hole. And I am sure to win!'

'Nadia!' I shout down, to where she sports with spear and underwater crayon – you have to cook your friends, and kill them too. Life is mired down – original sin awaits us on the plate, each pleasure's at the cost of someone else's life.'

'Oh fuss!' she cries. 'You want another world, and this is different, but it's still quite similar. I'll hunt and fish and cook – and you must do the same. Remember, you're the murderer among us ...' and she laughs and twists and streaks.

Peter's experts: another lot arrive. 'What's your game?' asks Nadia, fired up.

'It's spillikins,' the chief one says. 'Not the common kind. Scientific spillikins.' They lift and calculate, and draw the little timbers out, they bet, they laugh and scream. Then – 'Now, to nano-spillikins,' they cry, and sweep the table clear, they've only tiny screens, midget mechanics, they pile the rafters and the roofbeams high, and curse and triumph as they fall or stick.

Then, the boss turns to Nadia: she stands over them, she's naked, quite a show.

The guy says, 'My dear, have you a gill that you can show?'

'Not one!' says Nadia, twirling round and round: 'But this guy here,' she points at me, 'he's got one. On his conscience.'

'Nonsense,' I say, twisting around, 'I haven't got one. It was an accident. Besides, I thought you guys were engineers or such.'

'No, no,' the boss says, 'We're all restaurateurs. Maybe if Nadia here ... s'pose she had some gills. My! what a delicacy. As it is, we'll eat the rest she catches, and we'll throw her back.'

'This isn't what I hoped,' we both say.

'I can't open my eyes in the water,' I say. 'That way, every beast's fantastic, but I can't see any of them.'

'You breathe too much,' Nadia tells me. 'It's your fear of death. Be like me. Breathe slow. This is where we began, this water. I'll go back,' she says. That's no comfort, and there is no answer.

'These guys here,' says the boss, 'these melancholy warriors – they tell sad tales. They all have photographs of where the scene was young and fresh. It's an illusion. Not like that at all.'

The little lanes, bordered with stones, in pink and yellow, green weed and carapaces – 'jewel', they say, and 'lotus', all picked out. Do we make our way down those?

'No!' says Nadia. 'It's not here.' She puts on her lozenge suit. 'Whatever these guys, and Marcia, want, we shall not find it here, down in this hole.'

She weeps. I do not comfort her. Maybe she'd not want it – and I don't care so much.

I say, 'At least we're still together. Imagine – if you'd turned into a fish. Even a mermaid.'

She says, 'If you see me turning, just hug me close.'

That's not like her. Maybe she's laughing. Or turning.

'You're a bit dull,' she says, 'but at least you're stable. And we do have adventures!'

'Yes,' I say, 'but it's not danger you seek and fear. It's clear you're fearless, Nadia. There musn't be a threat. What is solid, in the world, what you seek, is curiosities, the curious. There's nothing worthwhile that isn't curious. Otherwise, it's banking or cooking – filling guts, conserving crap.'

'What can Marcia want?' asks Nadia, apparently agreeing. 'Another way of ruling the world, I guess. Assembling the shrivelled shards. We should follow the empty tracks.'

'It all sounds incoherent, Nadia,' I say, 'but right for you.'

'Oh, I know all about voting and civil wars, and tumours,' she says, gaily. 'And to me, it's obvious that Peter wants to send out chefs and maître d's. It's international cuisine, it can hit you five times every day. It never lets you go. Peter and Gill – they used to cook things up. Those polyps, *polpi*, poor things, being hoisted up their stairs.'

'We're leaving,' I tell the foreman.

'What!' he says. 'I've never had workers like you. Like her, anyway. I see you're not an athlete – the Turkish part is less transparent. But – this is a fine job, you know.'

'You know what they say,' I tell him. '"To be a productive worker is not a piece of luck but a misfortune." True once, true always.'

'You'll miss the spillikins,' he pleads. 'Mr Yin will be aghast.'

*

We should write to Marcia. Carina too – it wouldn't hurt. 'And mention Hubert too,' I say. 'People like being reminded there's a family in the wall. Say we need cash, we have a pineal eye, the eye of God. Sees everything, even when there's nothing much.'

Marcia's message comes quick, without the cash: 'Get on with it.'

Nadia says, 'This Turkish thing...It irritates me too.'

'Discussing the Ark with Gill one day, I said maybe Noah took on some hippogryphs along with all the rest. And pairs of hetero beasts are not the same as nursery cutes – some males are tiny, and the females swallow them...'

'Like you and me,' says Nadia. 'But no doubt you'll find your slot, my dear – for every penny drops. Sooner or later,' and she laughs.

'And then Gill said, the mountain where the Ark touched down was in Armenia, and I said no, in Turkey. And he laughed and said 'We are all Turks, then, but – I shall be Armenian.'

'And that was where the feud began?'

'No, Nadia. It's just that in the tale, we didn't come from Africa, we came from Anatolia. Everyone, and all the animals as well. On board no doubt there was some coupling unscheduled and not written down.'

'Well, I come from the fish,' says Nadia. 'They had a good time in the flood. And thereafter too – no nonsense about borders and mountains. Nor property. It's my gift for survival – like cold blood, you don't know when you'll need it.'

'You go round eating each other,' I say.

'I have plans for you,' says Nadia, 'Don't worry so much about being eaten. It happens on land too.'

No one speaks of imaginary fish, fantastic: there is no need. They fly, they walk, they hide. There's nothing quite material they don't do. It's true I don't care much about them, not any one of them – but if you must have ancestors, then fish are just as good as Anatolians, I'd say.

I see her, a fish, in my arms. Quite tranquil. Bigger than a sturgeon, looking up at me, with the one eye they show, not speaking. I see the rocks around, piled up, with green trees on top. A sea, a lake, blue and flat. A ploughman, plodding, not looking up. No one falling from the sky. Just Nadia, up from the depths – not caught, just lying with me, and relaxing.

It's quite a romance.

'I'm always on the right side,' says Nadia, 'so I don't need any order or ordering about. That's what they want, the good guys and the bad – order which comes from discipline and fear. Like school. I don't want that. Lead your life like it could be set to music, sung. That coloratura! Have respect for secret things – like, you're the Yakuza, I'm your bodyguard. Keep touching the cat's scrotum, bringing you luck for ever.'

'It sounds easy, Nadia,' I say: 'But – for us, it's philosophers and generals. And wondering why. What does Marcia want with them? And the bankers. Where are they?'

'Oh, people collect anything,' says Nadia. 'Bankers won't talk to you. What they do is secret, so they say. They're busy ruling everything. Maybe they don't even shrink when dead – they swell like marrows. Marcia – she has the passion, that's what counts. What Peter doesn't have.'

'I'm not sure,' I say. 'Suppose we go to Italy. They've had lots of both, the generals, philosophers. Pareto, Vico ... The universe is round, they're always

there, and then they're gone – but no! they're back again ...
the morning and the evening stars. Now, what can she
want with husks like that? Those generals too – off to fight
for Hitler in their cardboard shoes, to Russia – not harming
anyone of course, and then back home, those who
survived, all communists, repentant till the next ... Then,
there's Germany, and France ...'

'Enough!' says Nadia. 'There's no lesson there. What
Marcia wants is stuff that's dead, in tiny boxes ... She can
boast about them to her friends ...'

'People collect odd things, it's true,' I say. 'Pictures
of ancestors: of unknown guys. Statues of gods you don't
believe in, stone nudes, guns that don't fire. Landscapes
from wonderland. It's the abstraction that's beneath it all.
It's quest for wonders, mysteries you seek but knowing all
about them when you start. It's odd.'

'That's why it's fun,' says Nadia. 'They know, you
don't.'

Pandora's Box

'It's a vase, not boxes,' says Nadia. 'We know – Marcia
brings back what Peter's sent out. She's not collecting
trophies. She is collecting trouble. She'll spill them over
everywhere, and every night.'

'If we're fighting over order,' I say, 'it can go on for
ever.'

'That's why I do what I do,' she says. 'Although I know it's all in order, somewhere, everything. The rocks, the birds, the stars, the lives and deaths. No one's responsible, but it's ordered just the same. Buried coins, the axioms, the strings of stuff invisible. There it lies, you can't disturb it. You're born into all of it.'

'Marcia will disturb,' I say. 'And – bankers. They don't shrink, they rule the world, our world. So – they should be beyond the troubles.'

'Hmmm,' says Nadia: 'I don't think it works like that. Because bankers swell, because they don't talk to you, because it's all a secret except what they tell each other ... no, I don't think that excludes the troubles. Maybe Marcia can't collect those, the banking kind. Maybe theirs are bigger troubles, that won't fit in the vase. Maybe there's someone else above. Maybe they have friends still higher...'

'Why trouble with philosophers?' I ask: 'They are the harmless ones.'

'Oh,' says Nadia, 'It's their embroidery, the marquetry. All you need to know is how it's run and ordered. Philosophy will only justify – it tells you what you do is good or bad, then there's an end to it. They have no punch – the blow comes from elsewhere. You do what you will do. I know it all,' she says. 'Even the cakes – they turn to crap. But I don't think so much about that part.'

'Bankers? Philosophers? Not much crowd-pull there,' I say. 'You need to see the thin guys in grey suits signing death warrants – where are they? Your scene, Nadia –

there's not much romance in it.'

'It's Marcia's scene,' says Nadia. 'It's her Sans Souci. Then there's the war. I know all this, and I shan't serve. I'm the tree that bends before the storm.'

'I thought it was "bows before the storm",' I say.

'Don't be provocative,' she says. 'That way you'll lose the only friend you'll ever have.'

*

On Ashok's desk – a big green Ganesh, long tusks on his prosthetic head. Is this a fantastic animal, I wonder, or divinity with a handicap?

A guy with an electric broom comes in and out. Ashok makes a long call to his wife, a short one to a woman whom he likes.

It's clean inside, but not outside. We don't directly raise the question of the shrunken ones. 'You're one of Peter's men,' says Nadia. 'Tell us – what do you do with dead philosophers?'

'We burn and scatter, or we throw them in the river, like you've seen us on TV,' says Ashok.

'We're buying stuff for Marcia: curios,' I say.

'Marcia's evil,' Ashok says. 'Peter said that. Troubles. Who wants them? Provocation. Digging up the past, letting it spill out again. "You're lucky," Peter used to say, "You've got the Bomb."'

'I'm interested in animals,' I say: not true, but it's another track.

'When the Hunas came,' says Ashok. 'Those ruffianly guys that you call Huns – their chieftain led his army round a mountain road. An elephant fell down, down, into the ravine. My! What a squeal! The chief was so entranced, he threw another down. Then more and more. A hundred, so they say. Oh, what a waste – and just to hear those trumpets sound, as elephant and elephant passed over to the other side!' He strokes his Ganesh, its belly lounging: its little crown: its face expressionless. 'Fat Man,' he murmurs. Divinities – down the mountainside.

'Well,' I say, 'there's a lesson somewhere there, for sure. Aesthetics threatening your kit, I guess. Anyway, there you have them, in your tale: a general, a bit of philosophy, some music. And leaves no trace. Not him, nor any of them. Stirred into all the other peoples.'

'Off you go,' says Ashok, smiling courteously: 'Don't go gawping at the poor – there's hardly any left. We should have got to know each other – but, you know, I'm not paid to socialise, and I guess you've no cash of your own.'

As we leave, the guy absorbs our last dust in his broom.

'Fuck it,' says Nadia, 'that's enough guys, countries and religions. Economics, politics – that's the same all over. I'm not going into finance, and farming crabs, all that morality! It's that we don't have much to show for all our wanderings.'

'We have God's eye, packed in the egg,' I say, 'and that should be enough. The question is – do we do good to bring Marcia more troubles still? The eye – it's full of trouble. But how would she put it in her show? Then what?'

'I think there's a case for bringing back catastrophe. People should have it all before them, though I guess they always do. Besides, we've got our job to do, commissions to exact, all that,' she says.

'That's it! It's done!' I say. 'We've made our search. Adventures end with mass executions or a new career. We expect neither. Come on!'

*

We're back in the big city. Marcia asks, 'What have you got for me. How did you get on?'

'A rape and a beating. Not bad,' says Nadia. 'Quite typical. I knew he'd rescue me – he owes a duty. Then I had a swim.'

'And did you get to see inside Togon's closet?' Marcia asks. 'A general? A fierce blue spirit? Otherwise, the other two, Osman and Ashok – it's all stereotypes.'

I hold out the egg: 'We just found this. All-seeing eye. You need a brain, connect them up. Away you go.'

'It's that I really want,' says Marcia, snatching it. 'The rest I've got – should be enough. There's wonders done now, with these gadgets, all-seeing eyes, all-knowing brains,' and she peers through, like it was the seer's stone, a picture of the future on the other side. 'I won't say that you did well. But – if you've no cash, you don't collect, you steal,' and she juggles with the eye, as if she's separating white from yolk.

'We saw the conservationists,' says Nadia. 'Playing five-a-side. And Ashok, with his modern stuff. His bomb.'

'Don't be trivial,' says Marcia angrily. 'I bet Ashok asked after Carina. A marriage made in heaven, it would be. Alas, the girl's so absent. And her father ... locked up, like Bluebeard's wives. *Alles leben!* But that's no comfort, not to anyone,' and she hums an aria.

'You're in great form, Marcia,' Nadia says.

Nadia's pants – they're flared! She's gone far back. She's badly shocked, regressed. She says,

'The children. Where were they? We just saw ordinary powerful guys. No unicorns, no talking rats and mice. Everything that's new was hid, or maybe if we'd questioned ...'

'Yes, yes,' says Marcia, impatiently, 'I expect you wanted secrets to come out. I should have told you – banking secrecy's impenetrable. You needn't bother, needn't try.'

'I know your secret, though,' says Nadia. 'Marcia – you'll bring them back to life. Your shrunken dead. Marshals Napoleonic, Marshals Soviet. Every philosopher—'

'Yes, yes,' says Marcia. 'That's the plan. I'll play my flute. I'll be the Frederick – think of the Sans Souci, imagine the symposia. What fun! Those soldiers strutting, trying to be lent some army; defending, invading – think, what a wonder, to have them all – the thinkers and the strategists – all living and disputing. And with my eye, I'll make a panorama. No – a synthesis. Out of disorder, order will come.'

'It's horrible,' says Nadia. 'Even now they're always with us, philosophers, generals. The dead, the martyrs. But their condition is reduced, they are dried down. There must be room for new ones, for the life that's springing up.' She turns to me. 'You must oppose it,' and she pummels me.

'I'm not so sure,' I say. 'Marcia is good at hiding things – maybe she's as good at bringing them to life.'

'It's the past,' says Nadia. 'Bringing it to life – it's so repetitive. And the vainglory, the vanity. Over and over. Treasuring each word was bad enough – but now they'll all be here, setting us right. Repeating all of it. No, no, it can't be done. This is beyond collecting, it's vampiring.'

'Well,' I say. 'Maybe you're right. But Marcia was a friend – at least of yours. I held her door, was all.'

'Maybe you could cause an accident,' says Nadia, 'You are good at those, with doors. It can't be done by Yāma, you don't believe in it.'

'I'm not the type that does things twice,' I say.

'It's not a type, it's everyone,' she says. 'Twice, and twice again. Ganesh for luck, or Heisenberg – it all turns out for the best – it's inconfutable as well. Luck and order – what a pair! As for tumbling off the mountain path, well, sure, that's the worst of luck, but that will happen too.'

I remember Marcia's chicken legs: there's pathos there.

'You do it, then,' I say. 'It's your idea.'

'I can't,' she says, 'I'm a creative, that's my thing. Besides – ending it – what a boost to our relationship!'

'We don't have one,' I say.

'Of course we do,' she says. 'It's not psychology and depths, it's what we are and do. The rest was proto-feminism, the gazing into eyes and souls, the wanting unattainables. We're different species, you and I, so be content with that. Like when you thought I was a fish, not caught, but lying in your arms. And now, of course – doing what I want is good for our relationship!'

'Nadia,' I say, 'remember the adventures. They must have entered, somehow, into you ...'

'Those awful guys – though swimming was the best. Those creepy conservationists. And the rest – rapists and paedophiles! Some desk rat with his Bomb.'

I think back – on my project. The hybrid animals. And men. Putting the noble things, and the terrible, in one, glorying us and them, our versatility. In harmony, with variations, men and animals. Concocting them is our most creative gesture ...

'No, no,' cries Nadia. 'No! The fusion's false. These animals – hybrid, metamorphosed. It's not a joke, nor noble. It is art, that's all. I do that stuff myself.'

'What Marcia does, or what she hopes to do – it merely adds to what there is. It's nothing new,' I say.

'Exactly!' Nadia shouts. 'It's old, it's déjà vu. Think – this way you'll rescue Hubert. Maybe find Carina too. That hidden family – out it will spring from wall and from elision...'

'Liberating them,' I say. 'It doesn't interest me. That's an illusion too. The gangs of slaves plod on, they take their wages, some of them, that bind them to the next, and then the next, day after day, labour expended shackling future days.'

'That's infantile,' she says. 'It's that we could afford adventures, others can't. Now – remember Gill and Peter – what they saw in you was not a scholar, but a hitman. Go and see Peter. He is sure to bless.'

Peter

There's nothing on his desk. I wonder if he's wearing espadrilles. He says,

'Come to apologise, I guess – the murder. Accident.'

'No, not at all,' I say, 'You can't excuse an accident.'

'Well, Gill has gone where he has no opinion,' Peter says, and waits.

'Lots of things – have consequences. Unintended. Those – can we call them accidents?' I ask.

'Hmmm,' he says, 'Intention. That's a slippery one. I intend, I fully mean it – today I'll go to paradise. Why wait for the drear, the painful end? You see, philosophy and generals, setting goals and boundaries – and then the wars: they're full of unintended consequences, although there's lots of intention at the start. Take Nadia – she's for luck and accident. But then – she plans those silly cakes down to the silver bauble and the coconut flake.'

'Anyway,' I ask, 'how you doing, Peter?'

'Oh,' he says, 'here it's museums, galleries. Precincts of the classiest kind. And then – you know – there's guys, Fellows, that come and do their plans, and then go back. Our culture here's mixed in. Most of them are ours, will always be.'

'I saw Osman. Togon and Ashok,' I say, and he twists a bit.

'Yes, well, they were Gill's protégés, more than mine,' he says.

'It's Marcia that I've come about. She wants a past revived. The dead brought back, quite faithfully,' I say.

'Faith is a worthwhile thing,' he says, 'not to sound sententious. And science too. The grateful dead. It strikes a chord. You know, the dodo went extinct because it tasted nice. And when they bring it back – why, turkeys can live on in peace! I think of that first dodo crêpe, my gut implores, saliva trickles, appetite goes red. But let me tell you – in the past, we won a war or lost. There were no other consequences. Nothing by accident. Philosophy, instead – it had the longest consequences, most unintended, many fought upon. Now, we moderns switch it all around: the wars, the generals – they cause the accidents. Wars linger on, no one can tell if you have won or lost. It's strategy, you see. Philosophy, in contrast to the ancient stuff, now counts exactly zero. Now, Marcia plans to muddle this all up. The then, the now. So, what will count, and what will not?'

Peter has learned not to provoke, at least when he speaks to me. Muscles and ethnicity – he keeps quite schtum about them.

He says, 'Of course, there's always been a questioning about poor Marcia's family. She says they're all alive behind the wall – but if you can't see them, where's the proof?'

'Hubert is fine, where he is, or not,' I say. 'It's Carina I should like to see.'

'Ah yes,' says Peter.

He must be doing better, on his own, without the everlasting chatter with his friend. Poor Gill. He goes on, 'Carina – she's your unicorn, of course. So delicate, so scaredy, hiding behind those trees. Not like the others, fantasies that jump right out, and wave their attributes, and tell their tales, as you go on your way. You do not pause, you question them quite superficially, as you trudge on.

'And then – your quest fulfilled: mass executions. Promotion. Two kinds of victory – but where do all those creatures go? Yes. Carina, the unicorn. Of course, if you can't see her, she must be quite chaste and pure. Let's put those two together. Chaste and pure. How well they sit beside each other, on the couch, demure.'

'Well, that's settled for Marcia,' I say. '"Off with her head", your placet says.'

We gaze at one another, satisfied. I say, 'You know, the trouble with you and Gill was, the "ruling the world" thing.'

He laughs, and swings his feet up on the desk. Yes,

they're espadrilles.

'No,' he says, 'not rule. Just push the world a little nearer to the sun. For warmth, not extinction, of course. And now – no eternal return! Quite the contrary. Just giving guys cash to do their projects, then sending them out into our world. What else is there? Hope. That's what there is.'

*

'You needn't have done that,' Nadia says: 'Apologise. It's for patsies.'

'I didn't. To do that, you need feel guilty. I suppose. Or responsible,' I say.

'Well,' she says, 'You and your inner self can argue that one out. Here, take this for luck. The deed must be done – that's what deeds are for.'

She hands me the cat's scrotum. I say, 'You could market these. Even larger ones for those who need a lot of luck.'

'I'm considering that,' she says: 'But you can't rush these things.'

'Waiting for my life to start', as the song says. I must plan another accident.

En forêt – change of scene

'We went to eat out. She felt she lacked class. She wore a slippery dress, it fell down, revealed a nipple. It was a great moment.' I remember it sadly.

'It was class,' says Sara.

'So – then, she knew she had it. Off she went,' I say: 'Class.'

'Talking of revelation – you seek the truth, enlightenment,' Sara twists round to tell me. This is not the moment: 'But the truth – it isn't you. It's alien. You know peace, and boredom. That's you. We all think like that, are like that. At the tops – it's axioms. All sorted out. But no – that's solipsism. Things being themselves, and thinking about it. But things change – by not-truth, not-enlightenment as well. You're in the dark, your brain is going well. Then, you put on the light – the place is full of things you haven't seen. For you, they'd not even been there. First, though, you must find the switch ...' Sara talks on. I'm not convinced. She calls me 'that plummy guy', when I am out of sight.

We're at this fashion show. That doesn't offer truth, enlightenment. That's a relief. The joyful seamstresses ... no one complains. It's show. On the video, no one throws paint at Fendi's furs. It's reactionary, transgressive, liberating, racist. The models – haughty slaves. You'd stand no chance with them. You couldn't offer luxury: – that's pinned on their backs. Nor poverty. Maybe – hardship: – the North Atlantic in a leaking yacht, the baked beans overboard.

Unfashionable frocks file past. Now, it's the threatened animals in costume.

Why am I here?

'I'm rich enough to do exactly what I want. Except for tragedies,' says Sara.

China. Here, everyone wears masks, except the Moldovans, even to shop.

'You grow old,' Sara persists, 'Then, that's your truth.'

'This miasma you see around you, Sara,' I say. 'Forget it! Look! Food in vats of fat. Dogs edible in wicker traps! Take in the difference!'

She's stuck in her dark groove. 'I wonder why she wanted to be empress,' she goes on. 'The dowager. If that is what you are, the dowager – surely it's enough. At least the Chinese know that when you die you go to hell, and down there it's corrupt, just like up here.'

'Or even more,' I say. 'You need more cash. I hope you've got lots left, my dear.'

'Oh,' she says, 'I used to have. But now, I don't accumulate, don't spend. Just pay you to accompany. Be my alibi, do my dirty tricks.'

'The pine-marten was rather sweet,' I say, to distract.

'They only featured inedible beasts,' she says.

In the street, masks have whiskers, guys sport stripy tails and zebra wigs. Where do they come from, these people, these animals, searching each other out? Do they make things, or just walk, seeking nourishment?

'I see the old sage, before his wine bowl, laughing at his short life,' says Sara.

'No, there's deeper,' I say. 'There has to be. It's not just frames of people you leave behind in summer fields.'

'Oh, I don't have time for that,' she says. 'Romance! That's all I've time for now.'

There's colours, pinks and reds – not much fashion, though.

'Everybody here,' says Sara. 'Who doesn't sport a tail, aspiring to prettiness, has a diploma. Knows foreign languages. That's ominous. This place will last millennia. You make a person pass exams – that sets them on the path, for always. And speaking with another tongue – that gives them claim of ownership.'

'You enter in the spirit here,' I say. 'Not the spirits buzzing round. I mean, the game.'

'Yes!' she says. 'That's what I always missed. Being a friend, having a shape you could remember.'

'Don't despair,' I say. 'If you die here, it'll be a nuisance, an immense one. Then, everyone will set to and forget.'

'Normal, then,' she says, with satisfaction. Yes, she's stuck firm to her life.

'Is this the future, then?' she asks. 'And does it work?'

She goes on. Her questions – what answers could you give?

'I'd always had older men,' she says. 'People – people in reception – thought they were my fathers. They were pleased when they found the guys were just – old. Then came the turning point, and they were young, younger than you. Then – they were just you, fizzled out.'

We two – we alone look in this mirror: Sara, a painted lady, getting ragged round the wings. Myself, tall and postcolonial, stooping a little to hide the terrible things … seeking atonement, both of us, or maybe just a prize. Sara drops her jaw, making a pucker to conceal the teeth. 'People here avoid the glass,' she says. 'Doubling yourself's bad omen. Never know when you can dump your twin. Besides – there's no way of verifying, that what you see is true.'

'It's true, Sara,' I say. 'Only ghosts need reassurance that they're real.'

Three guys rush up, their arms and legs like barrel hoops. They pause, and then rush off.

'You see,' I say. 'Beneath the swirl, there's interesting guys. The ones that rob, others who wait in line to take the power.'

'No,' Sara says. 'You have a shifty look. They didn't wait to try some con, or hustle us down dark stairs.'

'They must have known you've spent your cash,' I say.

'When I was small,' says Sara, 'they sent me into the fields, gave me a billhook. It was to kill the wounded animals.'

'You're here to see the frocks, Sara,' I say. 'They've killed the animals. They don't need your advice. Now, they dress like them. It's all for beauty, Sara. Think –

there's a million artists, just in this city, I expect. No one will buy their stuff. So, they paint it on the sidewalks, on cliffs, float it down rivers, thresh it through dams. The animals – it's just the tender part, for walking round in ...'

'It's keeping it together,' Sara says. 'We should be behind that. It's telling that you're keeping it together, that's the trick, the hard bit. It's doing the stats. It's recruiting the guys that do the harsh things they have to do. We must hope. I'll buy a pin or mug, to celebrate.'

We don't find one.

I say, 'The way it goes, is symphonies. Then, it's lots of groups. Then, all the music's different.'

'That's quite an other thing,' says Sara. 'A thing will last as long as you can make it. Think of theatre, people sit for hours, and it is barely tonal.'

We've done with China.

'I'll take those ideas for frocks,' says Sara. 'Maybe start a shop. When I get home.'

Home, where the new bad things await. Guys here – they have it good. Very ancient, shopping for the new. A stupid thought.

'The animals,' says Sara. 'They should give a hint. They've been around so long, longer than us; before we plugged in our brains. So long they suffered and submitted ... They must have an angle, surely ...'

'They really moved you, then?' I ask, not much concerned. 'They were just pros, imported mostly.'

Now we're home.

I tell Marco and Britt: 'We made nothing of China.

Banalities. It was full of explorers like us. Looking for strange continents. But it was full, quite full. If they wanted to talk to us – we had nothing to say. I didn't understand it at all – though I don't know what that understanding might have been. Sara'd gone with me to see the fashions ...'

It was the last of her money. The day we got back, she slept briefly, and woke with her memory gone. 'Gone, completely effaced,' I say. 'She eats and drinks, and breathes. Then – nothing. She has nothing to talk about, as there's no new or old. She knows nothing – less than an infant.'

'That makes her the supreme bore,' says Britt. She shivers.

'No, no,' I say. 'Of course, it's interesting. It's like coming to America, without the Indians. It's being dead, and not yet born.'

Wonder, concern: we try both these, and others. I say, 'She mentioned the dowager empress.'

'Don't fantasise!' says Britt. 'She's old, she dies. Naturally, you feel some guilt. She isn't empress of vast realms. Her brain's an eight ball, that is all.'

'I don't like losing things, people,' I say. 'Even if I'm quite indifferent to them. Losing is a loss.'

'I want to lose Marco, and it's good,' she says. Marco turns away.

'It's like Sara's gone back to the start, hiding in her forest,' he says. It looks like he's been crying.

'Probably not as sensible as that,' I say. 'And you

can't speak of leaving your memory behind on the catwalk.'

Sara can't remember what remembering is. I say,

'She had what she thought was a hard life. She enjoyed telling us that.'

'Remembering and forgetting – they're our pleasures,' Marco says. Britt looks as if she resents her past with him.

Later, I get a call – Sara's run off. 'She's in the woods. This year, there's lots of berries. She'll do well. It's what she wants,' they say.

I often look out, at the trees. There's no sign of Sara.

'What was wrong with Marco?' I ask Britt.

'He was every straight girl's dream,' she says. 'If you want the same dream day and night.' She hums 'Livin' in the land of dreamin''...'

'What does he do,' I ask. 'When he's not hanging round with you?'

'You could ask him,' she says. 'I haven't killed him. Just sloughed him, like a skin. He was all over me. Now I'm a new snake. He did something with nerves. He got on mine. Some hospital.'

'Those guys – always on the side of life, until they're not,' I say. 'How'll you do for cash and space now, Britt?' I ask.

'We're all a team, I thought,' she says. 'Sara with lots of cash, Marco in your brains, and you translate ... there's all our friends. I guess we all help out.'

'You'll need more than that,' I say.

'I help you out,' she says. 'You're always asking – "in that street, what would you buy ... or see across that lake?" It's disconnected words and scenes, from books and stuff that's made of disconnected words and scenes. It's not an easy task, you've begged of me.' I say,

'China. That's what did for Sara. Those people busy, not asking us, not wanting any info that we'd have for them. The exercises – with their arms, their swords, with laths. Talking in all those languages, laughing and solemn. Bland, plotting, aspiring. Quite indifferent to her, her men, her memories. It made her cancel out. Those people's past – she'd got from picture books. There's nothing of a past that you can see, it's all been built on. Down underground, or washed away.'

Britt turns on me, 'Translation! You don't belong, you carry from side to side, you have no side, no tongue, no country. Fudge and bungle. Matricides, traducers of minds!' She seems angry.

'No more!' she shouts. How tall she is, taller than me. 'No more! No more, the cops, the robbers! No more, the being hung on hooks, the nostrils slit, issue of boots, issue of guns, issue of hats too small, too large. No more – administering the millions, the slice from this, the fingernail from that. No documents and no tattoos, no being loved or tolerated. No more the rights, the wrongs, the marching and the standing quiet and docile. No more! I want the new, the getaway, but not with him, and not with you, and not with millions more. I spit on you, the history you write, the photos that you take, your views, your daubs, impressions, opinions, anecdotes. Away with them – your piddling countries and their gods, the dreary customs, away the girls this side, the pigs' throats cut on that. Off with the boredom, off with the doing over, the dancing with one foot, the drumming with one hand. Away with where we've got to!'

We pause. I say, 'Sara grew tired of what was in her head. She left it behind. It was the only way. We only do what we can do and be.'

'Exactly so,' says Britt. 'Stuck. Like pigs – a horrible death, humiliating, at some cretin's hands. On and on, from being born to yielding up the soul you haven't got. Smile and say goodbye. Pitiful!'

'"We poor people",' I say. '"*Nur der Tod endigt ...*" – only death ends our bitter distress.'

'No, no,' she shouts. 'Escape, not death! The spies! The interests! The guys who give you stuff, then send you off to war. The priests who promise stuff, and send you off to war! The writers – give you history.... Marco – spying in your head, and gives you normal life, with him on top and grunting! I could convert, and fight the crap from deep within ...'

'No, no,' I say, fired up. 'You mustn't seek alliances, they do you down, they spy on you to see you're clean, obedient. Guys who want the revolution – just to keep some creepy foreign friends they've found on their computer—'

She interrupts. 'Don't trivialise!' she shouts. 'Translating is the worst! You spread it all around, you are the key the spies employ to find what happens on the other side ...'

'Finding out – it's all spying?' I ask. She ignores me.

'I'd be a Kodo drummer. The discipline, the sound, my body. What's more absurd, than beating drums, empty? Putting in and taking out – nothing. Air, vibration. Then give it up, renounce. Take the body, thin as string. Find my nature.'

'They didn't all look so ascetic, Britt, when we were over there,' I say.

'Fuck human nature. It's mine I'm after,' she says.

'Sara's not wise, Britt, she's demented,' I say.

'Well,' says Britt, 'I'm not. I'm a tiger. Are they demented? They don't have a book of rules. They may look demented, prowling up and down.'

'Yes, Britt,' I say, 'you're quite a bit demented, now I look. There's tiger in us both. I'm a destroyer. First you do it to yourself. Then you punish. That's not at all your scene.'

'No!' she says. 'Why even mention it? You don't know fuck, so you destroy. That isn't me, no, not at all.'

*

Next day, I hear her, early, clumping around the room. Can you make a plan – play the drums, and then start off again, invent humanity? Not as a scrappy couple, encysted with misogyny, misanthropy, breeding everyone, faulty from the off ... This time, just one. Britt. Not an individual, not a solitary, not sexed. Empty. No – emptied. No massacres, no memories, no things you've gotta fix.

'You're a flute,' she says. 'How you irritate! Every orifice you stop, out comes a different tongue. Translation! You're hollow.'

'You, Britt, you're a jar, in the woods. Hollow too, and proud of it. You fear a skill, if you had one, you'd think it flowed from you and left you dry,' I say. 'Now, do you want food brought, and left outside your lair – until you find what you can prey upon?'

'No,' she says. 'Just tofu. And chocolate. I'll be feral. Bins. They hold all you could want. The kids – wanted writing poetry, show-jumping; now, it's toting nightsoil. Remember that. I'll leave my daughter with you. Amber.'

It's a bad name: something precious – valued, at least – with something dead and nasty inside. It's a good name.

'Britt thinks only of herself,' says Amber. 'And Marco thinks only of her. So – I stay here, I guess.'

'I translate,' I say. 'I don't coax humans out of kids. Just conjure clean texts out of fusty ones.'

'Porn or jihad – it's all the same to you?' she asks.

I say, 'The fees are different. It's all a part of being grownup, reading about things.'

'Really, I'd prefer the woods to you,' she says. 'Until we small ones catch the fears, we're Amazons. Look at Alice – the danger and the perspective. Time liquid on the rocks. She answered back, she swam, came through. Those porous landscapes – like translations. Lying quiet in French, then eat some cake, swell up, you're drawn out gross – watch out! here come false English friends! Their stodge! Their podgy hands!'

'Maybe you could forage in the woods, Amber,' I say. 'You're full of matter, and the metamorphoses. No animal would eat you, and you couldn't catch one: you're too rubbery, too slow. You'd be Britt's familiar.'

'OK,' says Amber, 'you win. You're monstrous. I can't be trusted to you. Maybe I'll sometimes bring my cakes and have my tea with you.'

Britt says to me, 'Children are big and small, at the same time. You don't seem to know much about it. Is it too difficult?'

'She's continuity,' I say. 'That's why there's never anything that's new. Each tail is hooked to other tails. Dead the patriarch – why, here comes another, the muzzle's grey, the muscles overstretched ...'

'Yes,' shouts Britt at Amber. 'You're the flaw! The crack in the bowl.'

Amber shouts back, 'You're nothing but a pack of wastrels and egoists.'

'Treasure your resentments, Amber,' says Britt. 'And broadcast them all your life.'

'We've tried everything, Amber,' I say. 'I put the blame on capitalism. It's like those animals – one head's cut off, another grows, there's scales and then there's stripy skin. For me, translation is the worst. Not just the pay. It's sneaking, informing. Traducing. Taking some guy's words, denaturing them, decoding. You're the interrogator. Out comes something unintended by the guy

... In a language they had never known! And held against them. Banned, maybe. Or ridiculed. Without a greater or a littler good to justify. 'The snow is sticky as marshmallows' – there's the line ... you change it utterly...' And I talk on, but Amber isn't pacified. We must get rid of her.

'Yes, fuck off, Amber,' Britt says. 'We're not a tribe. No braiding of the hair, no poison for the arrows. We can't teach you stuff. Go off, and forage for yourself. We'll start again, and all the secret purposes, all the delights we find – we'll keep them to ourselves.'

Amber's appalled. 'Go, go,' shouts Britt.

'This is Greek!' says Amber, smacking her brow and trying to rend her top.

'She'll soon find living on the street and mooching stogies is not the fun they say,' says Britt, firmly. 'If we want to set up something new, we can't have smartass kids around.'

We didn't need gods to get us into trouble. They won't get us out.

'I'm off!' says Britt. 'Maybe other guys'll find the gadgets – build new sorts of friends, filter the air, all that. I can't. You can't. China didn't teach you anything ...'

'They didn't try,' I say. 'Not like old times. Once, the revolutionary guys, who'd found the upward spiral, the air vent ... they even paid you to say how great they were. And to spy for them as well. Now – in China, they're on their own, like it's always been: and so are you.'

'You can hang around,' says Britt. 'We enterprising

ones – we'll start from scratch. Scratch it will be,' she
laughs. 'You'll hear me at your door – gimme some milk.
I'll be the human on all fours, and furs. Inside – the
universal values: on the outside, visible – the claws and
fangs.'

*

The years of faking scholarship are left behind: the hope of
some paid spying job gone sour. I see Britt leave the city,
optimistic with her pots and cushions – off to the woods,
the forests. Living off the land, and planting beans. Men
look for gangs, women for some territory.

'It's terrible, frightening, when the cities go down,'
says Britt: 'You'd be crazy to stay around for that. Now,
I'll live like everyone else. Wild. No favours.'

'I shan't argue with you, Britt,' I say, 'though I
could.'

'Don't,' she says. 'You'll lose. I'll shout you down.'

'It doesn't end, sudden, day into night,' I say. 'Our
civilisation has an afterlife. You hang on. There's reprises.
Buildings get stood up again, there's processions, families,
parties in the street.'

'No, no,' she says. 'You can't have been around,
taken it all in. Don't you remember what we did to them,
the others? Threatened, chivvied – even bombed and
looted them. You think it's slow slow time for us? – and
you, a punisher?'

'There's always dada groups around,' I say, 'and guys

who always wanted to live rough and dirty ...'

'Their dogs! The smoke! The brown food and guys exploding with a drama, just to make a show – all like Amber, with their mouths,' she says.

I go on, trying to talk her deeper in to where she wants – I tell her, 'Britt! – in the woods, not all the animals feed us when we want.' She says,

'It's like those cities, where they worked – by day, no guys that you could see. All down there, below, down in the mine. By night – they pop up, in the bars. The forest – maybe it's a better deal. Although – that rain, comes through the trees, you wouldn't think it ...'

'If we hang on,' I say, 'there'll be new rules. Most will adapt.'

'Rules, rules,' she shouts, 'I didn't like the last – imagine if I'll love the new.'

I feel the same. I don't want the wilderness, is all.

*

Later, I see her in the wood. She's in a bothy, a bower. She looks overgrown, just like before. There's a group of watercolorists around, some not Chinese. All men – that seems to help their concentration.

I ask, 'Do you see Sara?'

'Sometimes,' she says.

'I don't believe you,' I say.

'Truth is treats,' she says. 'Like the plums in plumcake. Some that's so called has no plums at all, not ever.'

'Do these guys pay?' I ask.

'I do have fees,' she says. 'There's no furry animals left. I'm the next thing.'

'You are quite furry,' I say. Is this a way of life she's found? Unless we're experts, we don't ask the creatures what they eat. They can't have touched Alice's cakes and potions – they must have known it was a set-up. Britt asks,

'Is this the end or a beginning? It should be better marked. There's paths laid out all through the woods. Someone must have a destination.' She waits for me to invent an answer. I say,

'Maybe it was all starts.'

One of the painters says, 'There's tent cities all over – but this bower's different.'

I say, 'It's you that's supposed to be different. You need to put her in your context.'

'Oh no,' he says, 'that isn't art at all. The idea is, that she's the context.'

'She looks for something new. Everything,' I say.

'I don't want to be new,' he says. 'I'm me already.'

Li Xian, it says on his knapsack. 'I don't scent some mysticism here,' he says.

'It was animals that she was after,' I say. 'Not nature – that spills into laws, those don't account for disappearances. Nothing's wasted, nothing vanishes. The laws say that. Animals – go, and go forever.'

'She waits for something, that is clear. But she's lost something, too. Money, for sure,' says Li.

There's peace, the painters in their semicircle, fifteen angles on the oracle, Britt. Some message passes. Who is making sense to whom?

'I'm getting close to somewhere, but you guys – you don't come into it,' Britt says, although she turns her best side to the artists, buttons up her frock.

Then, there's a tootle and a roar. Some bearded guys appear. You cannot sort it out – it's 'Planet of the Apes', confusion everywhere.

'They're hunting her!' shouts Li Xian. Britt lolls her tongue at them, quite like a fox. That must be what foxes do that riles the dogs, the horsemen.

'It's all in fun,' shouts someone. 'They can't want to eat her,' and I think of Amber – it would make your mark to have a relative that's hunted through the woods, and torn.

There's guys all round, and hunting calls from every quarter – that's how they communicate, the huntsmen – or the apes. The trees obstruct your sightline.

'On, on, the artists,' shouts Li Xian. 'Pay no attention. Take a new sheet out, if they should savage her or tear her...' and he talks of Orpheus and his severed head, the seasons needing sacrifice, all that, with cultivated details I've forgot, though music comes in somewhere, and the horns are fretting on in three dimensions, and the guys are whooping too.

'It's all laid on, my friends, there is no extra charge,' the painters' leader says. 'Paint on, paint on.' And so they do.

'Don't move, Britt,' I shout. 'Just listen to the music.'

The guys on horses, with their pikes and billhooks – they circle, each move is musically endorsed.

'The hunters – they ride well,' says Li Xian. 'So did the apes. They'd probably been the Indians or the cowboys days before. But they weren't musical at all.'

'If they come closer, I shall sing,' says Britt. 'And if they tear me, I shall sing beyond my death. Maybe that will be the new, what I have always sought.'

'No political significance, none at all,' the leader of the hunt shouts out.

The painters stand: so tall, it's like the angels taking off, a mission. I see their work – some have Britt in manga-style, and some in pastoral. There's her in armour cap-à-pie, some nude with pubic feathers: some versions show Britt with sages round, and wine cups, some have her as an iridescent slab. A priestess, whore, a gardener ...

The hunters sweep around.

The painters – they unhorse the mounted predators. Those on foot with hunting horns – the artists wind the coils around the throats, they shout, 'Go, go, we're busy with our painting work ...' The hunt's dispersed, the danger's gone – and Britt says to me – 'I have had epiphany. Quite beyond words – there was the crag, the mountain, and I knew, that if I climbed it to the top – I'd look and see the fall, the depths. So – what's the point. Aspiring's better than arriving, and the disappointment.'

'What now, Britt?' I ask. 'The hunters have been hunted down, your bower defiled. You are a model, but ...'

'You owe me something. Now I shall collect,' she says. 'My display has run its course.'

'Nothing is owed,' I say. 'Not by anyone. What you see around's just small wheels in the large ones.'

'Those men,' she says, 'the painters, saved my life. I don't especially like them.'

'I don't suppose they thought of saving you,' I say. 'They wanted to finish up their pictures. They wanted you to stand, the wood behind. Then, what happened after – they were indifferent.'

'I know how deer feel. I'd like to say "the stag", but even fantasy's engendered,' she says. 'I sweated rank.'

'Britt,' I say, 'you won't find anything, no respite. That's your strong point. That's why you're a model. There's nothing in you anyone can share. You're the Idea, there are no replicas.'

'Maybe I should talk to Amber. Give her an example she'll repudiate ...' says Britt.

'You're not quite right to have that kind of past. Amber is past. Forget her, Britt,' I say.

*

I stumble across Amber. She's in a box, a shelter. Destitute, I think. 'Time to get up!' I say.

'There's no hours,' she says. 'They let us stay. It's a concession, it's a punishment. We do stuff – theatre, cleaning up. Stopping crime. Then we find a squat.'

'It sounds ok,' I say, not caring if it is.

'It's not like you, drinking in the new,' she says: 'China. The frock parade. Two women of the woods, one disappeared, the other hunted, saved by watercolorists.'

I say, 'It sounds more novel than it was. And Marco?'

'You know the Kafka story, the Mouse-singer? You did it all at school,' she says. 'Marco gave little bits of brain. To make the rodents sing. Just like they tried with apes. They feel we take from animals, this is our way to give some culture back. To make a bridge.'

'I'd not thought of Kafka linked with brains and surgery,' I say. 'Though it is true he had a line on torture, body shapes, that stuff.'

'You're out of date, and touch,' she says. 'Men are everywhere. They rent each others' soil. They plough for wheat beneath the ice, they use the sun to light up their tv. Stuff is flown up and down, to everywhere, the flowers, the fruit. Earth is a garden now, it's all for sale, and everybody digs. We don't. We are the only ones without a fork and spade.'

She sounds quite proud. I say, 'I know all that. And so the animals get brought in, fleshing out the show, conserved, dismembered, they give a limb, a snout, they get a rousing alto voice ...'

'That elephant head transplant that Ganesh got – it marked the way,' she says.

I say, 'That wasn't science, Amber. And I don't do agriculture either.'

'No,' she says, 'you translate. You ferry, carry over souls. Dead on one side, still dead when they arrive. Just for the fee. And a reputation, too – they say you don't believe in souls, some guys you dump...over the side, cold corpsy water.'

'The fee is tiny, Amber,' humouring her, I say, 'And you must take it from dead mouths.'

From other cartons, other guys crawl out. It is a jolly scene. I say,

'Look, Amber, translating is quite difficult if you don't know the languages. They say the primal tongue was Hebrew, that got overlaid. Now the guys say it's your brain, is all set up.'

'So,' Amber says, 'we're back to brains. Maybe that mouse of Marco's, with his brain implant, will start to speak as well as sing.'

'If it's Hebrew, how shall we know?' I ask. 'The guys that want translated stuff – they do so as they're ignorant – more ignorant than you. You find some Slovak, or a Bulgar – get them to give the drift. And there you are.'

Amber looks admiring: 'I always thought you were a prof,' she says. 'But now I see – you are a chancer. You're in my circle. Now, there's Sara, disappeared. And Britt – I see her there, at bay. Magnificent. The painters, with their box of paints, the battle with the centaurs – what splashes! Ultramarine, burnt umber, postbox red. That cadmium stuff. We did it all at school, of course – but now the epic's on some scrolls, stoppered up and underground. Those moulded soldiers, guarding the regal corpse, on the qui vive, the qui va là, a full brigade, mouldering left, right....'

'It all depends on how you see,' I say. I'd like to boast

of travelling, of postcolonial soldiering, of making accidents, every action for hire, spot cash. But then she says,

'This life – look how it makes my time run on ahead. It's speeding up, the clocks whizz round, I have a birthday every week.'

I say, 'My time doubles back. It slows, returns eternally, and once again, I'm where I left them, my fellows and my fellowship. The goodfellas. It all starts over. Those Chinese painters – functionaries on their holidays...Gill used to target them for a conversion. His allies, in the name of aesthetics universal. The old theories, values pinked and rouged – and out they came again ... Time slows, the clocks fall back, and I am younger ...'

'Look at me,' shouts Amber, 'You'd say I'm twenty, pushing thirty. Just a month ago I was underage and ignorant.'

It's true. Our ages rush to meet. It's opera. The spells unspelled. She rises from her catafalque, and I throw down the palace gates. I could be some rich guy, come to rescue her from carton city. Time, like a concertina, spreads its feathers, time past returns, time present exits right.

'Those Africans have bought Siberia,' Amber says: 'To grow the awful roots they eat. Chicago passes to Japan. Berlin's in hock to Uzbeks. Maybe we are one, a species monolingual – but, meanwhile, I'm sprawled here on the street.'

'I'd rescue you, of course,' I say: 'But what a past I've had! I didn't help one person, not at all ...' and so I think of Nadia, and her cakes, and Britt. Poor Britt – I stood and watched ... they say a deer will climb a firtree to escape the dogs. And I just watched ... it is the scientific turn. Britt didn't climb, nor anything. Just stood and watched: that's fear.

'Big bosses over there, in China – they all have singing wives,' says Amber. 'It has caught on everywhere. It is the common, the artistic touch. Pop, opera, even lieder – and there's males as well: the generals make up a consort, the admirals are into madrigals. Remember – cossack groups, the Red Army singing as it roamed? – well, now, song's everywhere. The spheres have jumbled into one another – comedians and jugglers, conjurers and stuntmen – all are voted in to parliaments. They lead, they rhapsodise, predict. Apologies for empire and for massacre – the scene is rich and ripe. And me – I croak. I fumble with the Indian clubs, I swallow gasoline, I can't spit fire...'

'Come, Amber,' I say. 'That rules you out of politics. There's other things...'

'Marco used to say, "consult the stars". But now he's mute. If the stars should speak – he can't. He would have been a leader of mankind, he sought the world behind the world, the picture that lies beneath the canvas, the melody beneath the pentagram ...' and Amber weeps.

'Amber,' I say, 'you've freed yourself from work – now, you've no idea what to do.'

'Your work – it's conning,' Amber says: 'You spin air.'

Nadia – she made things. Cakes you couldn't eat. Most things you can't eat. Self-portraits is one of them.

Amber's printed off a sign – 'hands off our arms'. I wonder if she means it to be funny.

'That's what you can do,' I say. 'A stand for ethics. My granddad used to shuffle to the Internationale. Those days, that place, you went to jail if you just knew the words. The Left. No punch, it's just morality. There's a history project you could do. So, that could suit.'

'It's news to me,' says Amber. 'The international. We're global now.' She plunges deep into her memory: 'You have no country, but you aren't a working man. Where does that leave you?'

'Amber,' I protest. 'It's not about me. I'm like Britt – an empty jar, left in the woods. You think in Uighur – I put it into Mandarin. That is all. No offence. No violence. Like I said – traducing, traduction. Being in between, I'm the grubby pig in the middle. Nadia used to say – people who make things, don't do sex. That's why artists don't have kids. They're up all night – like guys who're making autoframes. That turns you off women. And men.'

'When Marco operates,' says Amber, seriously, 'since he is mute, the mouse must give the orders. When you need the surgery – slip the animal some treats.'

'I don't need surgery,' I say. 'I see things clearly. And I tell them as they are.'

*

'Your secret's safe,' says Nadia. 'Those assassinations. Marcia sees everything, but she can't hear or speak. When you made history fall on her – those boxes, the collected stuff, the universal eye ... You stopped her, like she was a clock. Now, it's neither back nor forward. Her friends can go and wash her, if they wish.'

'What secret, Nadia? Forget it!' I say. Then: 'My! You're doing angry art.'

There's stuff so sharp, it cuts your eyes. Those tongues with spikes ...

'Yes,' she says. 'I got articulate. I hate the ones who don't appreciate my stuff, despise the ones who do. And I make lots of money – just by being furious ...'

She must have an angle, given some interviews. 'I spit on history,' she says. 'In that, no profit lies. Instead, you bet on countries going down, and everyone's your enemy. That way, you have some hope.'

'There's people run,' I say, and think of Britt: 'And some has humour,' and I think of Amber: her 'arms for the good guys,' and the mice in scrubs. I contemplate the world. 'The trouble is,' I say, 'we're not Chinese. They do what they must do. They do their exercise.'

'That's crap,' shouts Nadia. 'Culture and country? We travelled everywhere. It isn't so. There's natural humans everywhere. Didn't you see? And you – a punisher ...

'What we should be,' she says, looking round, 'is China. A place. Not to rival, but to complement. We can exemplify the things they haven't got.'

'Are we wearing the right clothes?' asks Amber. 'That's at least a thing we could get right.'

Britt wears a caftan – maybe the word gave Amber the idea – of Kafka. Amber wears a set of stripy woollen tubes. The colours of the tantra, though that shouldn't bother her. Nadia – all in grey – or just the black and white washed out.

'What do we have that they've not got?' asks Britt. 'Probably it's better that we say "we are all Chinese now". Otherwise, it sounds as if we have some plot or secret, or we are just arrogant.'

'We have the scream,' says Amber. 'The Chinese get on well without it.'

'Old videos, Amber,' Nadia says. 'Besides, I scream because I haven't got. I don't know what it is I lack, of course. In my case, feeling the absence is my temperament. There isn't content. It is sound.'

They look at me:

'We need you,' Nadia says. 'If we must kill or wound. Otherwise, you're just a bridge from there to here.'

'Nadia,' I say, 'we have our principles. We made our journey, set our provinces of meaning all to rights. We are accessories, one to the other. Remember that.'

The accidental murders .... it's the way you count the consequences – unintended, but predictable. They stay with you, like implants. The poverty – it gets to all of us. The wealth also.

'Accessories,' says Amber. 'That sounds awfully clothes-shop. One thing we can be, since in China they have eaten all their animals, or put them under glass, is haven. The fauna – they can share our food.'

'Amber!' says Britt, brusquely. 'The animals – they *are* our food. They never bring us eats, it is their destiny, and they accept. They eat each other, and in that sense – we are each other; in the scrum. And so, accept.'

'We must think,' says Nadia, imposing order, 'what they have and we haven't. What's left over must fit us, and be our speciality. Them – famine. Chivvying. The great helmsman and the unsinkable boat. Work. Unequal reward. There, in synthesis, that's China. And you're right, Amber, no scream. No Iggy Pop.'

'We have: the Grail. And – self-hatred,' Britt says.

'No, no,' says Nadia. 'Self-dislike, maybe. Dislike of others too – competition. Envy, perhaps. The good time, ever-receding in the trees, just like the unicorn. The good intentions; marches end in blistered toes.'

'I don't compete,' Amber objects. 'I show the way. "Arms for the good guys" – that is part of it. Don't prop up what falls down. That's another part.'

'You may be right, Amber,' Nadia says. 'But it's not an inspiration.'

'That's what I was,' Britt says, 'Inspiration. And they set the dogs on me.'

'Just bad luck,' I say. 'Wrong look, wrong place. You should have joined the game, the hunt. Like foxes do. They run. You stood.'

'Remember, Amber,' Britt says sternly. 'No light enthusiasms. "All desire seeks eternity".'

'I won't fall for that, Mama!' says Amber. 'I may seem an obstacle, a wall. But – I want to win some hands, not lose the money that I haven't got.'

'Enough!' shouts Nadia. 'We'll take Amber's crass ripostes as sparkling questions. Look on her positive side. But – we must avoid pushing ourselves on other guys. That's why Gill's head got hammered in the door. And – no dwelling on the history. That did for Marcia.'

My role – it is decisive. Punishment – of the unthinking, the unaware. I'd like another role. It is deserved.

'We could consult Li Xian,' I say. 'He saved poor Britt – though putting other guys at risk ...'

Li Xian says, 'It's all about order and disorder now. Probably it always was, the philosophy, the politics.' I find him working at his job. 'Green suits,' he says, 'And orange shoes. Will take the mind carry it away. But real green – apples and arsenic.' He buys the stuff, the cloth. That is his job.

'Britt wanted something new,' says Amber. 'But I live among new things. There's an abundance of them. She didn't want to look. If she'd connect with something – a country, an empire, just engage, then she'd be into politics, then, if she wanted, she could back away.'

'It's like Li Xian says,' says Britt. 'There's no "who whom", it's all about what drives the horse, and what will make it fall. The whip, the sugar lump – what it takes to make the cart move on, and not have the horse lie down. Some people – they have religion, or a history, and make alliances. Mostly they go to jail, or down the cellar steps. The rest is us. But now – we've made another start ...'

'They'll look like new green shoots,' says Mister Li. 'As they go off to work, the managers, in my suits. Like crocuses, the green, the orange.'

'What is order, Mister Li?' I ask.

'I've read accounts of Inquisitions,' he replies. 'In various parts. They knew what was the normal thing – what to question, where to be silent, things not to be spoken of.'

'Just conformity,' I say. 'Bowing the knee, so's not to bow the neck?'

'No, no,' he says. 'That's not decent, that's not just. Of course, you must dissent. It's that – you guys, don't stand for anything, except your wagon falling in the ditch. Your wars – they didn't teach you anything? The Grand Inquisitors – they didn't say they were infallible, and yet you thought it all could last for ever. Ruling over needy guys. As if it was part of normal.'

'If we are to stand for disorder now,' says Britt. 'What side is yours?'

'Oh, I don't take a side,' says Mister Li. 'I am a sage. I colour-code, I do not moralise.'

'Hey,' I say. 'When Marco's mouse dies – what then?'

'Marco'll be a silent father,' Britt explains. 'That's the best kind. I expect he'll be a loving one.'

'You lot should feel a little sad,' says Li Xiang. 'The useful bit of him expires. You guys – you'd do much better without psyches. They grind you down.'

'I'll make up for him,' says Amber. 'I'll be a voice, a waterfall, a canyon.'

What can she mean? Does she want to be a deep one, make us afraid?

'That Amber,' says Li Xian, looking uneasy. 'She'll lead her troop of warriors to their end. They'll end up in the stream, a mystic knot. Embraced. Their wounds diverse but eloquent. Some operas – they have the wrong ones killed, and in the sequel, you assume it'll be turned right again, but no – wrong names, wrong parents, or a curse that lingers on, that is the plot, the destiny. That's where she comes from, Amber. Her nasty dead thing, the prehistoric tumour, inside, a motor rumbling.'

'We're black birds,' Amber says, wildly. 'On a grey sky. Doing what we are, until we hit the wall.'

'Don't be portentous, Amber,' Nadia says. 'There is no wall.'

'That's why the birds are so surprised,' says Amber. 'They think like you, Nadia, that there's grey sky, but not a wall.'

'Mister Li – he saved me, that should be a proof of something good,' Britt says.

'No, Britt,' I tell her. 'You were torn. Torn apart by dogs. This time, the next, the time before. We're always there, where it's dictated ...'

'No!' Nadia shouts. 'Don't humour her! Don't humour Amber. Things change, entirely. Go on a different track. Take Li Xian: it's not conquests it's about. Not wiping out, exterminations. Suffusion, rather. Permeation. Doing deals, gathering in, a give and take, pretending that there is no core. No centre that you must protect, the brain, the heart of everything.'

'We're not the last people, Nadia,' I say. 'We could as well be. Alone, the four of us – and Sara in the woods. Then look at Mister Li, and all those people massed behind him. Step out, Nadia! Take Amber to a fashion show. Dress her up. The fantasy's the last thing to disappear.'

'I suffer so, with foreigners,' says Nadia. 'But I'll go with Amber.'

We, the last people, with regiments of others all around.

We wait for their return.

Nadia, Amber, they come back.

Amber says, 'We saw some kittens, little boys tormenting them. There, they don't esteem the cat. Some guys said, 'Don't moralise about the pain. Pay the kids, then you can abandon the cats behind your hostelry, and they'll be fed from bins.' And so we did. Now, they say those cats – one white, one black, one red – they gave their colours to the national flag, they march in front, and bear the banner in parades.'

'I don't like the sound of that flag,' Britt says. 'But the tale is good. Did you enjoy the frocks?'

'They're so stern on the catwalk,' Amber says. 'They don't speak. Nor even miaow.'

'They look like dead dowagers,' Nadia says. 'Come not to talk to us. Empresses of Lithuania. They show no pity – though some fell over.'

'Most things don't talk,' says Britt. 'Clothes among them. History too is mute, and States. Scrolls and bowls...'

'Yes, yes,' says Nadia. 'I know all that. Talking's no good. Remember, I was raped. It's Amber – she may presage new things, but meanwhile she's a pain.'

What must we do, we four – to make a society, a belief?

*

Nadia shows me a box of glazed and coloured things.

They're genitalia. Enamelled. I recognise baboons', a rhino's – 'Some are racehorses', trotters, genuine repros – winners in Hong Kong,' she says. 'I send them off to China. They bring luck. The guys, politicals and bankers mostly – touch them when they make a deal. That's where our cash is from.'

'It's a marvel, Nadia,' I say. 'The taste is so refined – you never take them out, just feel them in your pants, silent, they chase away the demons.'

'That's right,' she says. 'And unisex, of course. You take your pick.'

I say, 'Our economy is guaranteed by them. They're fashion, and they'll never pall. But – it seems that I'm the risky one. I have a past – you're trying to ignore your own. Britt is at bay. Amber's gone to ground. They don't have histories.'

Nadia looks hard at me: 'Your trouble is, they're

training animals to sniff you out, the guilty ones, or those just on the edge between intention and the act. Your projects were – with Marcia, not to dig up history. And with Gill – not to conquer with ideas.'

'You were in the game as well,' I say. 'Marcia wanted a rerun – of everything, the past, the wars, all that. Gill paid for Peter, sending out the missionaries.'

'You ought to make a record of it, that would be your task,' she says.

'I can't do that,' I say. 'It's contradictory. You can't reject the record, and then write it down.'

'Your stupid move,' she says. 'Was notions about the men, the animals, how they can fuse, communicate, ally.'

'Oh, I just made it up,' I say. 'It's all in literature. Guys chat to creatures, or become them. It's a fantasy, only the marginals are taken in by that ...'

'No, no,' says Nadia. 'Fusion's in! It's not a kind of music, no – guys want the attributes of animals, to join with them. There's so few beasts that's left, their characters and skills, they mustn't disappear. They fuse into ourselves ...' and on she talks. I don't believe a word, it's all a metaphor.

But then – of course! The bird that flies, hunts like a lion. The bright and docile genius – the gooselike thing that is all other birds – the simurgh. How often we have sought – a man, a woman, that is all other men and women. One we could obey and serve, and execute the ones that don't. If they're not found – then maybe the son, the daughter, has all the qualities, and more, of father, mother. And in turn becomes a father, mother ... Sure, we need a horse that flies: a tiresome mistress who becomes a bush ... We could have that woman if we became the labrador that jumps up at her on the road, if we were the rain that bounces off the sidewalk ... We'd go to war more often if we were a snake, a tiger ... on I muse, and Nadia says,

'Our brains are scanned and read, just like our mail. They say it's terror that they seek, but really – it's obsession that they're after. Obsession – it's the contrary of fashion. And they can snip it out. Kafka must have had prevision ... Those animals, the models, like the ones you and Sara saw in China – were they just animals? Or our desires? Our decoration...' and I grip the dusty scrotum that she gave me, that has kept the bad things in the wings ... wings on the flying donkeys, or the swan that penetrates when you lie dreaming on the shore ...

*

Amber says, 'Britt – she's the clueless battered one, you see them by the thousand, walking up and down. She thinks to find herself – and if she does, she'll see she's a lone stick, a pole without a bean.' Amber laughs, her little joke.

'Well, Amber,' Nadia says. 'What will you find, you and your team?'

'Nothing at all. The point's to seek out,' Amber says.

'What?' asks Nadia. 'What point?'

'Not something I'd feel like telling you,' says Amber.

'Remember, Amber,' I say. 'We're the black hole from which other Chinas spring.'

'Li Xian says it's dialectics changes things,' Nadia says. 'But physics's not his strongest point.'

'Li Xian says in China, it's all merit. You all compete, then what you're good at – like telling colours from each other – means you're good,' I say: 'What you're good at doing , is what you are, your goodness. Badness is all the things you aren't, and cannot do.'

Amber says, 'I won't compete. I don't want to end up at the bottom. I don't want to be that, be good at being there.'

'You are at the bottom, Amber,' Nadia says. 'That's where Britt has let you drop. Now, you must try being good at it.'

'The great idea's a fine one, but it seems there is a flaw,' says Britt. 'This merit – it's mere utility. It's what fits, just now. So – it's up to someone else, someone who decides what you will do – and that decides the merit. It's a decision, from outside.'

'There's no outside,' says Mister Li.

'It's like that Alice,' Amber says. 'Those were no quests. They were a test, an obstacle race. A quest is when you look for something that you know, not just tricks that end when you're grownup, an airhead still.'

We feel disturbed, Nadia and I, for Mister Li. He's shown initiative, and been our guide. He is unlikeable. He'll be no use to Amber. Amber's mates will pull her to the bottom of the sea.

'Our differences,' Nadia says, 'don't fit together. It seems four corners don't make up a square.'

'It's fortunate there's only four of us,' says Britt,. 'but being awkward shapes – it doesn't count for anything.'

'Fuck it all,' says Li Xian. 'I'm not a spokesman for the world. Finishing the picture, is the thing – the angrier you get, the more they sell ...'

'Yes!' shouts Nadia, 'That's where the edge comes from.'

'Hoo hoo hoo,' sounds from the forest.

'The wolves! The wolves are back,' says Amber, joyfully. 'Now we'll see running – and what fun! Enough of whimsy – now the business starts.'

'It's Sara,' Britt says. 'Let's ignore it. She can't be helped.'

I can't be sure. I put an arm round Nadia, and she twists away.

'Hoo hoo,' comes back, 'Hoo hoo.'

*

'You and I,' I say to Nadia, 'are stuck in our improvised selves, doing eternal things. We won't change, but Britt is rattling down, the shale slides with her, over her. Death will demand we make a reckoning. Amber – she'd do well to join the cops, or lead a movement – brash and intolerant, with a cuddly core of bigots. She'll warm their interests. But – we looked for meaning in it all, and fell back on our own significance.'

'My work is a movie,' says Nadia, 'my life – a long novel. Two dead media. That makes me furious. It's a burr beneath my saddle, that drives me on, it's a suffering that makes me mute.'

'Nadia, your work is awful. And your life has never been as crafted as you say,' I tell her.

'Amber's movement's going well. It's hard to be subversive. Most things fall down by themselves. The guys that set them up just hope to die with gold coins in their slippers,' Nadia laughs. 'The people Amber leads – they mostly want the same. Dying rich. The grandees' epitaph. But – she's indifferent to all the bumbling stuff – climate, overcrowding, no air, no food. It's all turned into scams. She wants no one to have to shovel crap to get her food. It's an alarming pitch. She's for the species – it's pungent and usefully vague.'

'There is no species, Nadia,' I say. 'We're everything, all hundred species, but something vital lacks.'

'We can feel shame, repent. That's novel,' Nadia says.

'Poor people outside their doors with their throats cut,' I say.

'That signifies nothing,' Nadia says. 'It's not even punishment. There's no discrimination. And the moralism fits you bad, like Li Xian's suits.'

'It's bodies that don't fit,' I say. 'Amber says "Variety lasts better, fruits more, than uniformity. It doesn't matter what the variety's of. That requires, that is, a kind of uniformity. It doesn't matter what the uniformity's about." She got that from Li Xian.'

'Li Xian's a tailor,' Nadia says. 'He clothes the naked emperor. The emperor is always naked, underneath his clothes. We line the streets and we imagine him – clothed and naked. And in bed with everyone.'

*

Then, something terrible happens.

'I've realised,' says Amber, 'that everything is coming to its end much quicker than before. The Romans – they went on for years. They brought a war, won, then promised peace. Now, you must promise much much more, and dig and ration. Then – there's me: I've got these people following, they hang on every little thought. Suppose ... Li Xian, his homeland, what if that comes crashing down, or splintering apart? What if there's no renewal? What if you promise stuff, and then you can't come through? Suppose you promise peace – but then it's war? A civil war? A long one, a worm's tunnel?'

'Well, Amber,' Nadia says, 'you don't seem very bright. It's always so. War – the great lottery for individuals. For the big guys, it's a fix, all preordained. What will you tell your acolytes, the legions on the web? Sit tight, until my next remark? Prepare to tough it out?'

'I don't do sex,' says Amber, 'but – I do have dependencies. I need the huge ideas, they must keep rolling in. Mine is an empire, made of thoughts. Men, some women, I can cling to for a while, and milk their brains.'

'It's serial childhoods,' Nadia says, but I see she'd like to be Amber's guru, for a while. 'And – my work's not awful, just conservative. How do you live the artistic life? It all ends up boring you, then stored in cellars. That is cruel. But you must learn to love it.'

'Yes, conservative, Nadia,' I say. 'That's it. What we did back then – the voyage, the discrete assassinations – it finished up a phase.'

'It represented a phase,' says Nadia.

'Of course,' I continue, 'that's why you're angry. All that is over, you were a part of it, it's gone along with you, and there's nothing you can save of it. You live with all the damage suffered. Religion, the gurus, the guerillas. Fetishism too, accumulating. Ruling the world, as if it was all profitable, the people good, grateful, docile. All that's done with. We laugh, of course, to think of it. Some people ended up quite beached – Sara, Britt. Gone in among the trees.'

'Poor Sara,' Nadia says, 'She bet on fashion – the new, on and on, everywhere: really, the old returning, some fresh fard, the impersonal, the unsold, unwearable, unsaleable. And now – there's this terrible thing, you say.'

Amber's network – means she has her fans, can tell them what she likes, but never leads parades. I think it's easy times, she says it keeps her up quite late, typing the messages.

I look at her messages: 'In choosing Anatolia, Noah

had a prevision of the Prophet. Maybe he was one. His drunkenness – being taken with the spirit. And how did the animals know where to walk to, to be happy and in the right place? That mystic trip – was it water, or air, beneath the ship that survived the end? I think he absorbed the animals – those that were left, the ones the others ate, those procreating, taking the souls of the sterile ...'

It's beyond Mickey Mouse, beyond Alice. There must be metaphors hidden like plums in the cake you have to eat.

'It's a disaster,' says Mr Li. 'We must catch up – that's the aim, to replicate the leaders as they fall and sink. Food, the big army, harassing the stragglers. But – we're chasing failure. It has happened, and it will, over and over. You overtake, and then there comes – eternal return of the problem you can't solve, the lesson never learned. And so it happens, each time, faster and faster.'

'Is that the terrible thing?' asks Nadia.

The Solution

'There's a pattern,' says Mr Li. 'I cut out suits – patterns are my friends. But – you run ahead, you reach the limit. Over and over. You start again. Have you overcome the obstacle? You vote, you vote, more and more of you, more often ... and are the answers right? Are you content? Are other guys – the minorities, smaller and smaller, still they shoot up, the neighbours you are doing down – they don't vote with you ... so, you reach the wall. There's the obstacle it doesn't help to vote about.'

'This is heavy stuff,' says Nadia. 'My lucky genitals – they're cheap, they're works of art. They work, on all the levels. They work more, the more you guys are touching them.'

'How's your Mandarin?' Li Xian asks me, ignoring her.

'Oh, I can unpick the pictograms,' I say. 'It's mostly bowls and scrolls, a touch abstracted.'

'This scroll,' says Mister Li, waving a greenish bolt of stuff, 'hypothesises something new. It's animals. How to incorporate ourselves in natural lives, not eat nor hunt, but taking on their strength, their cunning. Of course, the author, the sage is dead. That's how it goes.'

'You're a collector, Mister Li? That's bad,' I say: 'You'll be defrauded. It doesn't even look old.'

Oh no, I think, another book that solves it all. The more it justifies your projects, the worse it is for everybody else.

'No, no,' says Mr Li, 'it isn't old. It's not for "people of the book". Rather "guys of the scroll".'

I unroll my work, what he's given me. It's harder than it seemed. I say, 'Nadia, I need a pictogram that I can strip down, disassemble.'

'I know the right man,' she says.

'It'll cost,' says Clancy. 'Silver, platinum – or plain white metal?'

'Silver,' I say. 'My client pays.'

The pictogram is beautiful. I'd put it on my desk. 'Make me some more,' I say, and we unroll a yard of scroll, and make a choice. The first one – 'Maybe it means "solstice",' I say. The parts are like birch twigs, old auto parts, laid on the floor.

'Maybe it's all a metaphor,' I say. 'See – "metaphor": that might be made of meteor and amphora, meaning the lightning's struck the wine.'

Beneath the text, I sense there's other texts. An Indian, a Persian one. Derived from trading horses, I've no doubt. 'This stuff you do with animals,' I say to Nadia, 'No sex would be involved?'

'That would be gross – there's maybe sensual friendships, shifting of awkward shapes, no more,' she says. 'Look – on this coin ...' and there's a tiger, underneath a parasol, a row of fish: rich dignifiers. To sell, to eat?

Clancy has made a family of pictograms, they click together, smooth, like dice. We unpick them, slot them into one another, make up new concepts, slide the seasons into buds and shoots.

'It's quite impressive,' Mister Li agrees. 'I could have Nadia sell them, put them on desks, and such. For managers.'

'There's every kind of story hidden here,' I say. 'Wise counsels, ways of life, an opera or two, and living happy for a while. You guys did well to build the Wall and try to keep things to yourselves.'

'Forget the Wall,' shouts Mister Li. 'It didn't keep them out, it didn't keep us in. Translate! Choose some other language that we know, and let's get on! Ignorance is not a wall – this way we'll maybe save the world, and overcome ...'

'But, Mister Li,' says Nadia. 'You can read the stuff that's on the scroll. For you, another language doesn't serve, it's all before you ...'

'You idiots,' he shouts again. 'I must communicate. It isn't words, it's landscapes, it's some worlds you'd have unbuckled here, set out like cogs and shafts – like Cadillac transmissions unfastened on the tiles ... Find me a plan that doesn't crash, good at the start, without an end.'

'It's all about the past, though, Mister Li,' I say. 'If there was project, clearly it was failing even then. Failing from the start.'

'It's maybe all about the future, then,' Nadia says. 'Proceed. Put everything together – on the floor is all of nature and activities, like playing flutes and fulling cloth and shearing sheep. Just raise it up, and tales will take their shape, and after comes construction ...'

'Yes, yes,' says Mister Li. 'Don't be deceived, don't just collect and sell these pictograms. Go to the next, decisive stage ...'

We think of Marcia, and our warning 'don't collect, and don't resuscitate'. On pain of invalidity.

'How about wonderlands?' Nadia asks: I think she's conning me. Amber has a wonderland, with hosts of followers, all plasma to her Alice. No one saw or helped

Alice as she had her fantasy. Then it concluded, cured into mortality.

I remember something like – 'hunting in the morning, fishing in the afternoon', and in the evening, being critical critics – but that's hard on the animals. It seems you must be in a forest, with a sea or river close. No factories, industrial parks. Organised in bands, except when you become a critic, when you're alone against the rest.

Li Xian looks hard at me: 'I wonder if I picked the best,' he says. 'Maybe you were better at revenge, and dodging who comes after you. A soldier's life, without the hat and boots.'

*

We go with Mister Li. 'One of my factories,' he says.

There's rows of guys, making his suits, grass green, goose green.

'Amber goes down well in this place,' Nadia says. 'These guys are keen on her, her mind turns on future things. She's sure the present will pass on. She makes her cash by dropping hints – some shoes, a suit – it's not quite ads, but nearly so.'

'These people,' Li Xian says, some sadness in his eye, 'Are all completely normal. You two are not. That's why I respect them, and need you to unwind the scroll. They know the future's coming. You seem not convinced of that.'

'I bet they've all signed up to Amber,' Nadia says.

'They'll all have my genitals in pocket or in a purse.'

'I'd like to see the sheep,' I say. 'They make the cloth.'

'And then we put them in a stew,' says Mister Li, laughing, and put out. 'Now, what does the scroll say?'

'There's this tiger, and the sage watches closely how it hunts. The tiger starts to give him tips. They make a band together. Closer and closer they become – the tiger lights the nightlamps with his tail, they sit and laugh together at their differences, the tiger sleeps in bed, alongside the philosopher-hunter's wife. He's treated as their son ...' I improvise.

'Yes, yes,' says Li Xian, 'that's nothing new. OK, they're close, there's plenty chapters more to come but ...'

'I know,' I say, 'you want something that's big, not just a flash of comradeship. I wonder where the tiger slept – the side, or middle?'

'Yes,' says Li Xian, 'something for when we hit, and so's we don't. I see our limit, incised now – these places where we make the suits, hi-rises. It's all the same trajectory. Old stuff: just replication. Like in the scroll – the generations rise, they stand upon each others' shoulders. Sometimes there's a relationship, while you go hoeing up and down. A bigger empire, then the crash. Thinking you're good, and everyone can be like you. And so – we try another trick: – translation. Here it doesn't work, so ship it out. From here to there, the place indifferent, until the guys turn sour. Then you move on. You shift your orders to another tongue, so quick you can't see it move across the lips. Tell him, Nadia,' he turns to her, 'It's not the shift from language into pictures that resolves, nor into numbers ...' She shrugs.

'Dance was the key,' she says. 'Except our legs – they won't accelerate, not for ever. Even with the tablets – they reach their limit, hit the wall. Mister Li – you built one wall, then you spilled over. But after, there's other walls, of sound, of light ...'

'We're nowhere near those yet,' says Mister Li: 'After the green, there's plum and cherry too,' and he is cheered by that.

We leave the factory, Mister Li says he's many more.

You can't see mountains here.

'This must be near Hoboken,' I say to Nadia.

'No, it's Radio City, where the mouse works,' she says. 'Li Xian says that you're the Master. It only means you're best at telling the story. I wonder, does he know you'll have to pay for all those accidents? It's because of fabulous animals, the project that you never did. Peter thought it promising – though in the end we always end up at the start.' I say,

'We could travel, Nadia, with the scroll. Telling its stories, looking for Li Xian's answer.'

'Yes, but it's not love. Or even sharing rooms,' she says. 'It might promote my charms ... If no one's interested, it will light up my anger too.'

No, not love – but who suggested that? That's not everything it's all about. And – the fabulous animals, the metaphors. Everyone is trucking them around – they're commonplaces, plaster casts in imaginary gardens. 'No, Nadia,' I say, 'forget the tales, the mythic beasts. You must believe in them, not try to solve some puzzle. Those guys – they don't believe. We saw so many things, but not a super animal, nor yet a human turning into one. There's that mouse, of course, but that is science. We ought to sell those silver pictograms instead.'

'Of course,' she says, 'that's best. I'll do the selling part. You're more the abstract type. Invent some story for Li Xian, and I'll take on the pictograms. I'll cheat you, but not much, and nothing personal.'

Li Xian – does he want to save the world, his empire? It seems as yet anomalous, and premature. I have more claims than him to be a saviour in the bud – I'm with the unfortunate, struggling, like them, to get away from them. I'm even quite a revolutionary – at least subversive. A coupla accidents – those can be forgiven, even celebrated. Compared with Amber, I'm an action man. Her calls to arms – that move no one. She has no substance, sits and sings invisible upon her branch. It is her forest, miniature, not like the hairy wood concealing Sara, Britt. And others too – there's Carina, who I've never seen. Maybe that is love ...

'You could pretend you're with the girl in the wall,' says Nadia, 'Carina.'

'You're nothing like her, Nadia.'

'That's not what I said. You don't listen,' she says, 'No one listens, or they'd live through some idea, not having it all end up in parliaments and gallows.'

'You're too conservative, Nadia,' I say.

'It's Li Xian, firing you up. That's a downer from the start. He's a clothier. It's walking up and down in different clothes. He wants his crew to run for ever, nothing more,' she says.

'Maybe you're right,' I say. 'You've suffered more, that makes you right more often.'

'You'll give suffering, to them, as they gave to me?' she asks. 'It burns me.'

I'm amazed. 'You're not like that,' I say, 'Vengeance, fury.' I suppose she is.

'You must do it,' she says, 'to every one of them. That's your task.'

'I went the classic way,' I say. 'Know yourself, control yourself, raise yourself. I thought I was at the last stage.'

'No,' she says, 'forget the opera stuff. You're at the first stage, always. Vengeance, to order, carried out on others, at our command.'

The dark. It's not so bad. The light, perhaps too much praised. Britt and Sara chose the dark. Gill and Marcia – they were people of the light, they hatched, they had their hour in the sun. The light, it's not so great.

'Where are you intending to end up, Nadia? At an art fair?' I ask.

'Oh,' she says, 'I can't think of much else that I want to do.'

Before us, in the line, there's a guy – on his knapsack, says he is Deng Yan. He could take a last seat on the bus.

He's reading – the title says 'Platonic solids'.

'How long you been here?' I ask.

'For ever,' Deng says. 'Is that your mate, the tall one, with the dusty hair? Her bottom's withered quite away. A bad sign, that. That way, the exit's proximate.'

'Oh, I'm quite estranged from food and drink,' says Nadia, joining us.

'The water and the food – they aren't good here,' says Deng. 'I harvest woods. My job. We've planted trees, you get a syrup from the leaves. Food and drink – the problem's solved.'

'There must be water somewhere that's involved,' Nadia says. 'And animals. But he's the one who likes them,' and she gestures at me. 'I just use their genitals.'

'Of course,' says Mr Deng. 'The animals is our competitors. Most of them, we do not need. It's food and water they are after. It was simple when we only had the phoenix and the dragon, some monkeys to remind us of our ancestors – but now, you dig, and there are millions. Tiny things, all brown and slime. We have to keep them from the woods.'

'I'm not that keen on animals,' I say. 'Their wary eager looks, those polished eyes that size you up as eats.'

'They've had their day,' says Mister Deng. 'Or if they haven't, they must try a little harder.'

'You'd maybe like to buy a pictogram,' I say, showing our leaflet: 'You see, "Spring", "Combat", "Eternity". They can replace a clock. For a translator, just contact me.'

'No, no,' laughs Deng. 'Now, there are kits. You make your own from struts and spars and rings. Yours is too difficult. It just does synonyms.'

'Enough!' shouts Nadia. 'I've hit my wall! Useless to go on. Who's left, among the trees? Our friends?'

Mr Deng salutes us, takes the penultimate place on the Greyhound. Nadia and I, we can't leave separately.

We watch the wood, while we wait for fresh transport.

That seems a mountain lion, among the bracken on the fringe, his dusty coat the colour of powdered gold and snuff, he stares at us, an eye – it seems to wink.

'Oxide of arsenic,' Nadia says. 'From the water. Their fur takes on that shade.'

'It's always been like that,' I say. 'Maybe it was Sara that he ate. Or Britt ...'

'Or even both,' says Nadia, brightening up. 'What a tale, if that were so! Our friends! Beats anything that's on the scroll. Amber could moralise about it to her friends, her followers.'

'See how well it integrates, that lion,' I say. 'Doesn't miss the mountains. Lopes in among the treacle trees.'

'You can't be sure,' she says. 'Assimilation, or digestion. You couldn't ask our friends how well they fitted. You've no more luck now that the beast has swallowed them.'

'New life,' I say. 'They carry on, renewed, and even noble. Ladies into lion. It gives you hope.'

'You speak so easy,' Nadia says. 'The words bypass

your brain. Just think – you'll be the one to bring my glass, the last one.'

The glass – I think of the all-seeing eye, the eye of God, we brought to Marcia. One of the many eyes, circling up there. Glass eyes. Watching, as we scutter up and down. 'No, no,' she says. 'A simple glass. To drink. Water, with its charge of arsenic, will do for me.'

'There aren't sufficient lions to do for all of us,' I say: 'At least, your art will live.'

'The sphinx. I see myself as one of those,' says Nadia. 'As for my art – it's in the world. It circulates. It's nothing more to do with me.'

'Eternal return. That's what Li Xian had hoped we'd go beyond,' I say. 'I'll try, Nadia, I shall try.'

She drinks the arsenic. It will take its time. She says, 'I sold my luck.'

I say, 'If you had given it away, it would have been the same. Li Xian will make his suits – plum blossom, and the plum. The apricot, the grape. Imagine – cities of some millions, all the guys in colours – maybe at most, he'll leave a buttock bare. A game, some fun.'

'You could get a job with him. You weren't suited for Peter's fellowship. Besides, unfinished projects, they're the best,' she says.

'I know all that,' I say.

'Will I all be eaten up?' she asks.

'You're much too tall,' I say. 'Don't think of that.'

'I'd make the lion ill,' she laughs. 'That's like a story from the scroll!'

'It's difficult to make those stories out,' I say. 'The lion is used to eating rotten stuff. Don't think about it, that is not the end.'

The wait is painful. No enlightenment. Perhaps the wrong person stands in line for punishment. I put out my hand towards her.

'No, not that,' she says.

THE WHITE ROOM

'Tout être humain est donc éternel dans chacune des secondes de son existence.'

Auguste Blanqui, quoted in Walter Benjamin,
Das Passagen-Werk

'If I could start over ... there's so many stones to be deciphered.'

'I could have bigger breasts. Catch a bigger fish.'

'Not so. Even if it's only "could have" ...'

'You chose dull work because you're dull. You must accept.'

The animals – they bite, they scratch. In cases extreme, they eat. It's all they know of intimacy.

'I won't leave this house,' he says.

'It's my house,' she says. 'Legally, you're crap. Go study old civilisations. You're related to them.'

It's just.

That's the justice you look for, and live in. The best you can have. Look at toads – they mate, hundreds of them, with one specimen, quite overwhelmed. Stags, with their harem. Not to speak of sultans, with theirs.

'Stay with me,' says Mimmo.

'Wow, great,' he says, 'I knew it would be easy,

being fixed up.'

'Tomorrow, you'll find somewhere else,' Mimmo says: 'Now, the market.'

The stalls, wandering round, it's like a stomach. 'Oh no,' he says. 'Those poor animals, not all quite dead.'

'Don't try to save them,' Mimmo says. 'Think "sacrifice".'

'These books ...' he says, going in amongst them. He sniffs deep – French tobacco, old Soviet glue. 'I don't read,' he says. 'Everything outside, around – it's too bulky to get inside,' he tells the girl who'd sell one to him. 'You're so neat,' he tells her. 'Uncut, narrow, smelling so new, almost tacky still ...'

'Come on,' Mimmo says. 'This is how you ended in the garbage. Being yourself.'

'My job, classifying stuff. I should tell them I'm giving up,' he says.

'What's the point?' asks Mimmo. 'You're not there. The way to handle it, if you can't manage what's around you, is to be radical. Accept reality, project another one upon it.'

'You make me sound apart,' he says: 'I'm more in control than you are, Mimmo. I just cancel traces better. They want us to have relationships. Lots of them, all sorts, for tolerance. Then they go round so fast, like horses on a roundabout ... Learn to eat gherkins from a jar, learn to be Buddha. There's no end to being normal.'

'Well,' says Mimmo. 'The normalisers got it wrong. You're not.'

Animals, when they play or let it out – they don't shriek, attract the predators – they just roll upon the ground, look up at you, and wink. Us animals – we can't do that.

'Where are you?' Mimmo asks.

'Oh, I'm rooted here,' he says. 'There's the Bir-Hakeim bridge, the trains; beneath – Kabylia. My people, some of them. Others in the deserts, in the mines. All over. Dispersed throughout the world.'

'You must go further,' Mimmo says.

'It's not you want me out your room?' he asks. 'People, chased from their land, hassled by the cops, it's everywhere, we all have part of that. Justice comes through war – you'll have heard that, Mimmo. It's not false. When the gods die, it goes on, all of it – not hope. It's physics.'

'Don't take off!' says Mimmo. 'No flights of hot air, no balloons. If you leave your wife, your mother, if they throw you out – it's quite normal. It's what the forces of our destinies want us to do, to be. We're ants, we're everywhere. Underground and in the trees. The universal species, we'll become – we'll take – the lot. Then sit and wait.'

'Well,' he says, unappeased. 'What if a solitary wolf comes knocking at your armoured door?'

'I'll shoot him through the keyhole,' Mimmo says, 'Straight through his yellow eye.'

Gay Paree. How the words shift their shapes, their partners. Friends.

'Look,' says Mimmo. 'I don't want you around. Understand. Go and fight for something. There is choice. Territory, history, justice, work. Each has its army. You've ancestors all over, no doubt relations too. All grievances are just, and unresolvable. Your mating season's done. Fuck off. Here, take this.'

'No!' he says, 'that's not me. It changes things, utterly. You lose your distance, the "he" becomes an "I", and it an "it".'

It's a dog. It's nature, but the coddling kind that you don't want.

Here's an emporium, 'Au paradis'. That is what we want. The doors open when you step up on the plate. Everything, the world – sea urchins and agarbatti. I push the dog inside, the doors are closed. The dog's too light to open them. Like all of us, it will find the butchers, eventually. We stare at each other, it's surely a moment it will remember. I'll forget it, likely, but I'm free. 'Farewell,' I do not say, 'Fuck you twice, Mimmo, old friend.'

This city – its works displayed, like an exclusive watch. Guys pushing rails of suits. The grey slates, like scales on pangolins. The glum passages. Melons, flowers, faces, all of marzipan, glazed. Do they all make movies here? Or cut horses into steaks? How busy they all are, and sharp; small sharp brains inside those nifty clothes. You need some drinks, and in the bars, they're extras from some rousting movie, gangsters all assured. *Blousons*, eggs hardboiled.

'You look sad, pensive,' some stranger stops and says.

'I just lost my dog,' I say.

'Buy a bottle, party with us. You're sure to find another sad.'

I take the bottle up the stairs, where she had said. All the doors are silent. Maybe the party's sitting on the floor, eyes closed, thinking about Bergson. Maybe they're all younger than me. I leave the bottle at the top, the shabby place. Help the poor, they say.

Maybe I'll go see Effi. She abounds with life: she says, 'I'm an immigrant. Perfectly integrated. I understand them all. I hate them all. It's democratic here, so it burns, no sad greys wandering round. Run and run ...'

I say, 'They're bringing back the tsar ...'

'There's always tsars,' she says. 'Never the same one.'

'I'm a classifier,' I say. 'I just need a place to stay. There's always work for us: sorting the good, the bad, rough and smooth, the sane and sick, the odd, the even, round and square. Faded and perky. Do it to all materials,' I boast. 'My! How the people need us, to tell them what they've done.'

'Well,' she says, scooping her feet up beside her on a bed. 'If it's life you want – look in the fridge.'

'Maggots don't bother me,' I say. 'They don't put me off. They warn us, but there is no need. The quick, the dead. You don't have choice, it's not democracy ...'

'How you talk on,' she says. 'Share my bed. If you

have dreams, don't pee in them.'

Underneath the woollies, there's an attractive being, I am sure. From some part of empire, now still going on, or before. Russia, China, America. Into those, everything fits; she's a pupil from the big class, class of all classes.

'I do animals too,' I say. 'Classing where they are in the chain. Everyone gets some points.'
'Where am I?' Effi asks, wriggling.

'Not at the top. That's where there's nothing left to eat but lookalikes. Further up again, you must consume yourself,' I say.

'You class horizontal, and by vertical too. "Do no harm", that must be you,' she says, admiring.

'All is left just as it is, it's true, frustrating, sure – but then, it's only work,' I say. What does she do? I wonder.

'I work with animals,' she says. 'It's low as you can go.'

Sell? Stuff? Butcher? Train? Guard or release? Every pleasure's there, every one is covered.

'What's in it for you, Effi?'

'I seek their spirit. There's nothing for me in it,' she says.

'Nor them,' I say. 'It's nonsense. Which world d'you think we're in?'

'There's the revolution here,' she says. 'That must be going on, sort of. If not – those thousands gone, the speeches … Too bad. Sure, it's there. You need to cock your head to hear it.'

We try. I'm humouring her. She cries a little. Maybe I

do too. Things are dire.

'There's guys who pass through here,' I say. 'And fights ...'

'Nothing to do with you,' says Effi. 'It's about religion. In the end they pay me what they owe. We should discuss your rent. A full bed costs you more than empty ones. What did you think! And your fantasies – all free.'

'That's fine,' I say. 'The mystic stuff about the spirits – that was troubling me.'

'You don't believe we have a spirit?' Effi asks.

'No, Naturally not,' I say.

'Well, the lesser ones, what we call animals. They must have one. It's a compensation. You see it in their eyes. Mine's such a dirty job ...' she says. 'Not that it helps, or counts.'

'I'll find the money,' I say. 'It's respect.'

'People don't like me,' she says. Her face is pinched, in its frame, like a palm outward turned. 'But they love having sex with me. It's quite consuming.'

'So,' I say. 'I'm in your bed to guard?'

Perhaps some day, release?

'It's better than gratification, whatever you think that is,' she says. 'Mine's what they call an active life. Animals by day, lovers by night.'

'Well, that's up to you. Your problem,' I say, uninvolved. 'There's that revolution going on. Maybe you should step out on to it.'

She takes me to where she works: it's an emporium, Le Mange-tout. The window says – 'Bush meat:

Sacrificials: Halal, Kosher, Christian: Fireside and working: Agnostic and other: Taxidermy.'

'I'm so sorry, Effi,' I say.

'They don't know which class they are,' she says. 'It's the demand. That makes it clear.'

'If you have faith,' I say, at a loss, 'it must be tested.'

'Oh,' she says, 'it is, and how. The pay is pitiful.'

My seeing where she works seemed to have excited her: there's scrambling in the bed. 'Effi!' I say, 'don't change the game once the hands are dealt.'

'You can't just let those creatures do as they want, giving them rights at birth, letting the big ones eat them all,' she says, panting.

I say, 'Remember what Engels said. The bourgeoisie has its women in common.'

It isn't relevant, it seems, but calms her.

'You should go over the globe, help my business, and pay your debt,' she says: 'It's all right – it's business, not trapping and hobbling. You could be suited for it.'

It's a way out, certainly. A way in, too, a new life. And yet ... It isn't me. She's misread me. I'm respectable. She doesn't recognise the type. All those religions, those cuisines for carnivores. She's truly universal, serves them all. How she must pray, as she does her work, whatever it may be.

How terrible, to take Effi's origins as reasons for her moods, her fancies. Perhaps she comes from somewhere where they're slaves, or hunted, discriminated, their brains stunted, caged with malice. She was born with rights, they say. Suppose she has a history, and I haven't known? What if, in my ignorance, I'm prejudiced? Revolution was supposed to stop all that, even in France. I say, 'Effi, don't get me wrong. I'm maybe not the desperate case you think. Perhaps...there's something in your past, identity, that seeks revenge, a rectifying, justice?' 'No, no,' she says, 'I'm from a place I can't go back to – nothing more. We had a revolution – quite the wrong kind.'

I say, 'If we were Russians, centuries ago – the drama! Serfs and seigneurs, the modern at the gates, let in or not, the poetry ... salons and duels and leaving for the capital. There it was, history laid out – the revolution! There it comes! And now, us – we signify so little, big themes sound on above our heads ...'

'I think it's right, precisely, about us,' says Effi. 'We are exactly us, here, as we are. We are the wood, fresh felled, the carpenter shaves off a twist, away, away – a pile of baby curls. And what is left – it's always us.'

I leave her, in the middle of her muddled life. I travel everywhere. Settle accounts.

Here – the people have blue teeth. 'It shows they voted,' Neville says, a gross Englishman, Effi's agent – 'Don't you want to look inside?' he asks.

'No, no,' I say. 'There's big crates and there's little ones. That's all I need to know.'

'You ship stuff out,' he says. 'And you are Effi's girl. There's been a pack like you.'

'With me, it's crates,' I say, 'and Effi – well, it's hit and miss.'

Neville expands. 'I farm things here,' he says: 'Nature's so profligate. Think of those turtles, panicked, let down by the welcoming sea. And frogs. What you need in places like this here, where you can sell the topsoil, and what's underneath, and have the ladies walk the world to have the chance to clean your house – is weedy guys, aggressive ones. No warrior types, with empty heads. They must hate real good, and back it up with prayers. The hunks and hulks – the plump ones – they're a trap. They'd keep on selling what can find its price, like me. No – when the rebellion comes, the ratfaced pockmarked ones, all the disfavoured – they will have their day. They'll stick my head upon a lance, and burn and sing, and bring some rigour in.'

'I didn't see you as a revolutionary,' I say.

'Because you don't look in the crates,' says Neville. 'You're just another squeamish Effi boy. You don't know history: when the waves are taller than yourself, you let them sweep you off. You have survived. And then you don't.'

I have a meal with them, Neville, Paola. She's tall and blue and out of place, a delphinium. It's meat – I don't look in the pot.

Neville unlocks a wooden door, there's chicken wire so you can see in. There's guys, quiet, staring at their screens. 'There's Effi's boys,' says Neville. 'You can't let them out. They'd not survive, they don't know how. They do the books. There's poachers too, who'd take them. There's not many trained to sit before the screens.'

There's a movie playing on a bigger screen, quite silent. 'They have their fantasy, of course,' Neville goes on. 'It's Effi. My, but they're loyal! And they think – Paris, the capital. We play them Liebelei. Max Ophuls.'

And the singer – yes, she looks like Effi, and she sings on, in silence, you watch her mouth, her white skin. You'd like to be inside.

'They like the rough stuff too,' says Neville. 'About the Nazis. Those guys had faith – quite the wrong sort, of course. Effi's boys – they identify with the French, the revolution betrayed. Of course. It lets them off.'

You watch the mouth, and think of hooks, and being let off them.

'These guys,' I ask. 'Their business is all Africa?' 'Don't think of continents. It doesn't work. Think "worlds",' says Neville, puffing as he puts the padlocks back. 'Think "simultaneous" – it all goes on at once – the stuff revolves. It's markets, quotas, futures and pasts, the ores, the trees. Your animals – they serve; and all beliefs and needs are satisfied. You want a monkey in that chair – well, here he comes. We have the monkey mountains here. My! Are they glad to get a proper home. A lion to keep the burglars out? A snake to stopper up the draughts? Lemurs to light the path – those red sporgent eyes ... And eats! The thighs, the ribs – how the running sweetens, softens them...'

'The lady Paola,' I ask. 'She stands so tall?'

'The consort Paola,' Neville corrects. 'Lot of couples

work like that – one fat and hairy, the other, insidious like a sheet of tin. It's all thought out. All the anomalies. It's like the gold – laid down where guys are poor, and kill each other just to delve in holes. And then it goes where guys are rich, who lay it down in vaults. Now, tell me there is no intelligence at work! The distribution ... it instructs. That's what it's for.'

It's hard to contradict. If you don't want it so, then let it be. That dog ...

Neville grips my arm: 'You – you're pretty cold. You don't communicate, or claim some species similarity. I like that, though the other guys ignore you. You are Effi's type.'

He takes us, Paola and me – into a patch of jungle. 'This nut here,' says Neville, 'it was a favourite food. The guy who used to eat it – he's been crated and shipped out.'

The flower's a ruby, and the nut is teak. I gulp it down – I'm in a cylinder, the walls tattooed in red and green. The sides expand, it seems it is a lung, there's churning down below, two kidneys hang like purple plums. There's a trachea, up to the roof, a chimney – it might be a still down here, there's bubbling, smoke, a heaving, and a crisscross of emotion, breaths that come and go, the ribs that creak – oh no! I think, this creature has a sentimental life ... it's Liebelei, there's to come a duel, a suicide, and I should leave. I kick the single lung, a membrane roars and squeaks, a pibroch – but it coughs, it snorts, and up the gristly pipe I go ... a gaping mouth, a tooth ... and there is Paola, laughing as she cradles me.

'Naughty, oh naughty Neville, with his English japes,' she says, and holds me tight against a papery breast. 'The animals, they know the scene, they're used to being swallowed and regurgitated, sucked in, spat out – it's all the same to them. But we're not used ...' and Neville laughs. 'There is purpose there,' he says. 'And wisdom. Every animal eats that fruit. Even those who'll be extinct...'

He winks. Could he be that animal? Or think he is? Could it be me? Is it wise, to avoid the fruit of wisdom? Just doing what the immediate dictates, straight between the eyes. Like animals are said to do. Yet – you can't say that something hasn't left them wise ...

'It's all a game,' says Paola, cuddling me. 'It's just the way they fall – the dice, the cards. It should refresh, to know there's nothing you can do ...' I'm still terrified, shaking. She strokes me, tickles me, calls my name.

'It's just,' says Neville, 'Justice. You had no house, no territory. All you had, is still intact. You've not lost anything, no one has stolen from you. No one insults you, no one makes a monkey out of you. There's no injustice, indeed – now, you have knowledge, wisdom. That's what I'd hope to bring. Knowing how it can be, how it ought to be. Once you're inside – you can tickle the trachea, hope you'll get spat out – it's quite a reflex, automatic. It's Effi's shop, emporium, all over. Luck. But where all round there's exploitation, prejudice, slaughter quite indiscriminate, assassinations planned – you could attain, instead, the wisdom of the fruit ...'

He needs to instruct me – I'm not sure it's for my good. The wisdom is – it's chance, the data as they fall on you, give universal meaning to each instant.

He says, 'The revolution you're always mentioning. The poor, oppressed – you know, it's always misrepresented. If it happens, or does not.'

'Misrepresented? You mean betrayed? Falling over its own shoes?' I ask.

'No. Misrepresented. What I said. The actors, the script, the intentions and results,' he says, irritated.

'Writers, you mean? Inscriptions?' I ask, thinking of the tombstone forests.

'No, no,' he says. 'Everyone. Their hopes. I see the larger frame. What I want is what I've said – stripping out and shipping. The great chain of consuming. Eating, if you want the arrow-word.'

'I'm not sure I understand,' I say. 'Nature! Nature!' Neville shouts. 'We big animals – we have made it so, created! It's all ours, what we are meant to be. Nature is what we want it! We can eat it, if we want!'

'Effi looks for spirits in the beasts,' I say. 'I don't think there are.'

'Of course there are,' says Paola. 'Everyone has one. Even you, I'll bet!'

'You know,' I say, gently, as if they're a pair of cretins. 'All this shuffling things about and making us all comfortable ... the stripping and the shipping out – they say it's overdone, we'll all come to bad ends.'

Paola pushes me away. 'Sacrifice!' she says. 'It's in

our blood. It's what distinguishes us from all the rest, the other animals. The rite, blood, sacrifice. Oh, if they would only call me ... Rejoice! Rebirth, purity. Millions of us, extinguished and extinct, then – millions of years to wait, calm, dark, what luxury ... A new life rises ...'

'They won't call just you, Paola,' Neville says. 'They'll call everyone. That's what gives our end its greatness.'

'I don't just classify,' I say. 'Any idiot tells the difference between a large box, and a small. I know how the world works too! Duels, vendetta – they're a family matter. Spits and spats. Valhalla too – the stall closed down, gone out of business, watch the space, if you've the time. But Paola's into something new. Our time, our space and destiny ...' and Neville turns away.

'You find it hard to take things in,' he says. It's not a question. 'Paola didn't invent a thing,' he says. 'It's what there is. It's happened. Thing on thing, and after, thing. Now comes the time of sacrifice. Better get used to it, and stamp and dance around. There's no Nijinsky wriggling there, in that tight yellow skin. The music will not stop this time. This time, the sacrifice is not a rite – it is for good. It will be tough, but we are tough,' and he pinches Paola's arm. She doesn't wince.

We think about it: then he says, 'I'll take you round the world, we'll do our work. Effi wanted that.'

'Shall we go everywhere?' I ask.

'Not sure of England,' Neville says. 'I've never gone. It's all about the Scots.'

'You seem English to me,' I say.

'They're so aggressive,' Neville says. 'Then, there's the Scots. The English took their language, built those military roads to keep them down. All those Scots have is rocks and rain. They did resist – they're called Wee Free, that everyone derides. Religious. Bullies. Insults from everyone. A great injustice done, continuing. And the English, well, they all came in from Denmark, pushed the rest aside ...'

'I don't know about all that,' I say. 'But there is usually suffering all round.'

'Of course, of course,' says Neville. 'Yes: as Hegel says, we all must have our argument. But then – the English go off round the globe, their armies everywhere, at someone else's call. No, it's not my thing.'

'Paris isn't innocent,' I say, striving to make the peace.

'No, there's that too. But we must go somewhere. Trade, moving things around,' he says. 'If I could be something else, I would. Some creature. But even kangaroos – they do no harm, and when there's lots, they shoot a bunch.'

'It's all suffering,' I say. 'So, you stick by your free trade.'

'Suffering. You're right. Get ready for lots more. But – trade: it isn't free, you know. It costs as well,' he says.

We have reached a confine, there is silence. 'We shall journey with my cousin. Regina, from Brazil,' he says. 'No Paola?' I ask him. 'Oh no,' says Neville, 'she doesn't travel.'

On the road. I hear them, Neville, Regina – in the next room, if we have two, in our bed if not. They make a noisy love. I hear them singing out: quite loud, like Jorge Ben – 'Take it easy my brother Charles', and 'Xica da Silva', as if they're making fun of me.

'I'm glad you're travelling with us, Regina,' I say. 'Paola is a fine spike, but ...'

Regina's the colour of teak. 'Everyone fantasises about Brazilians,' she says. 'And it's quite justified. Paola's too stiff to come around the world, to where they're stripping out and shipping in.'

'Regina,' I say, 'you've got class. Paola doesn't.'

'Yes,' she says, 'I do. But not for you, you cheeky boy,' and she pinches my arm, quite hard, I feel there is a bone inside. I'll not forget the pinch, the 'cheeky boy', in all my life – it's worthwhile living, just for that.

'Regina has a magnificent *sillage*,' Neville says. 'High quality candlewax and moonflowers. You should keep downwind.'

We go to China, India, Indonesia. There's ships that ship. Animals – some live, some dead, like us, says Neville. Regina lets some pretty ones out of their crates, to run upon the quay. We don't know what will happen. Off we go ... 'I wonder ...' I say.

'You're soft because you think there's virtue in it,' says Regina: 'The guys here are all hard, because it works, and if they smile at you, behind their eyes, your skin is flapping empty, drying out so's it can patch their roof.'

'The guys we deal with,' Neville says. 'Stand on that shadowy line, that runs between the benefaction and the crime. It's history. You drain the swamps, mosquitoes come to town to dine on you. Action-reaction – you did it all at school.'

'Then there's Effi,' says Regina. 'I bet you think of her, you two. There's no reaction there – she seeks her kind of peace. Not scuffling with you.'

'What kind is that?' I ask.

'The earthly paradise, of course,' Regina says, 'Unattainable, but – so desirable.'

'Desire's a whim,' says Neville. 'An American thing, I fear. Me – I make no promises. When there's stuff to move – I help it move. Take my percent. Sometimes the guys who trap and dig – they live in paper boxes on the slope. When things go well – those same guys light cigars with golden bonds and live in villas on the hill. I claim no credit, and I shed no tear.'

Faster it spins, the world. The seas have vortices, like pockpits – you can see the luminescent wrecks down there, seaworms as thick as cables, mariners with gills, and Neville says – 'I've never felt the globe so round before, everything sliding eastwards, then it surges back again. Hold fast! – although you can't fall off – the air is thick, it pastes us on!'

He has a taste for poetry, our Neville, so it seems. I ask Regina, 'What is there in all this for you?' and she says, 'Oh, you can see how well he sings and how he screws. What more can humans want? Voyaging with him, there is no pain, he pockets his percent, there's no cadavers of a human kind, just crates and ships, and stuff that looks like soil.'

The gold, the teak, the ebony – that's not up to me. Here is my crate of sacrificials, sheep and goats together. Then there's crates marked 'science'. 'Caged'. Life sentences for all, some long, some very short. 'Of course, he lands, wherever there is flat,' Regina says. 'He's not a Dutchman, excluded from the ports: and, from fear of falling, Neville doesn't fly. Then, there is home, where Paola prepares the sacrifice.'

'You don't believe in that, Regina?' I ask.

'Oh yes,' she says, 'but – I don't take part. All those human bodies, made inedible – we're the only ones to think of that. I'll dance upon their graves, to tamp them down. Not the samba, though. Something more foxy.'

'Shipping these beasts to Paradis – I'm doing Effi good?' I ask.

'She keeps the gate,' Regina says. 'Is all. Brain not required.'

Neville brings a guy to meet us. 'This is Alvin,' Neville says. 'I don't know where he's from.'

Indeed, how would you know? His girl's called Kitty – she talks with clicks, like all our sailors. She wears warm slippers, heather mix. 'We're here to cheer you up,' she says. 'Alvin will help. He buys up land, and digs and sucks. And when it's done ...'

'We'll mine the stars,' laughs Alvin. 'Sacrifice is out. We may need fewer of us humans – fewer species too.

There's lots that sit around or swing in trees, they don't contribute much. We'll make the stuff we need in labs,' and as he talks, the scene grows lighter, and the sailors gather round. Maybe we'll find a port where others talk in clicks, and they will put on slippers too, old age will crease and crumple them ... and Kitty laughs, and says, 'There's last resorts you know! My husband was a Dutchman, such a bore, forbidden landfall. To rid myself, I ate him, not to economise, but to bring us both eternal peace,' and she shows us her pink palms and nails, the Nordic red inside her mouth, and we laugh too, and Neville shouts, 'A jest, a jest! We needed that. The future is secured.'

I say, 'My dog – if he'd had wings, he'd be an albatross,' and no one understands, but how they laugh, and laugh.

'Let's live on an island,' Neville says, 'and survive each other, and the world.'

'Everything is almost islands, anyway,' I say. 'Besides, when you arrive on one, you think of boats to get you off, and we're already travelling on boats.'

'Yes,' Kitty says. 'On islands, the animal you catch could be the last one anywhere, and eating it could bring you out in spots,' and Alvin laughs and says you'd need some spades and maps, and preferably slaves to dig up all the gold. We stare around, we think of the song – 'Are you satisfied, with an average life', it seems that's what we have, we are.

We take another boat, to go look back at the shore. It is what people do.

'Look!' says Regina. 'The scarlet sky! The air: it's musk – or is it gas? Smoke? Incense?'

We're not good at weather.

'The sailors stayed on shore,' I say. 'Maybe we can hear their clicks. A roister ...'

'No, no,' Kitty says. 'That's not clicks – it is artillery. Oh no! It has begun. Rebellion. The last, the final, the decisive war – it starts. We're on this ship, all stuck with different hopes and interests. And we can't land, for fear...'

'It is the time of sacrifice, like Paola thinks, so maybe I should say farewell to dear Regina, prepare for endings sour,' Neville says, and weeps, 'I'll call the captain ...' but there's no one there.

'These old ships,' Alvin says. 'They sail around the world, there's no one up on deck, they're playing gin below. If there's no crew, it makes no odds. All is settled somewhere else. For fear of pirates, who have dug up all the gold. Their hobby is to pickle skulls ... It's best we go below, and let them fight it out on shore.'

'That goddam Dutchman,' Kitty shouts. 'We'll never find a port where we can dock,' and it is true – we travel on, and everywhere there's flame and gas and buildings sliding down.

'No people! Let no people on,' says Alvin. They're swimming out. 'We must decide which side we're on. Who knows where these people stand? Use these poles to push them off.'

'What if we're on different sides, the five of us?'

Regina asks.

'Don't lift out animals,' shouts Neville. 'They may turn on us. Besides, we've plenty food in cans ...'

'Effi's supplies,' I say. 'Let's think of that.'

'Oh, there's the zoos,' says Neville, 'and lots just running round the streets. After a while, trade will start again – it's always so, things settle down, they always have. There's fire and ash and ice, then seaweed blooms, and we march out the slime again ...'

Alvin's robust, and fends off everything and everyone that's hoping to be picked up.

'On shore, it may be justice they are fighting for. Can we abstain?' Regina asks, and Kitty says, 'No! What if it's the start of the long war that ends it all, and we'll become the dinosaurs and leave our bones in hardening mud?'

'Oh, that's just Paola!' Neville says. 'Our lot can last out for a hundred years, and then we shan't be there to care.'

Then there's the coffins, floating out. 'Look,' says Neville. 'They're open. The eyes. A last look at the sky? See how they float!'

'What you think?' asks Alvin. 'They make coffins so they sink? Holes in the bottom? It's nature, that is all.'

'Well,' Kitty says, 'I hope the guys out there have sense enough to burn their crappy shacks and go to live in villas higher up the hill.'

'That leaves things as they were, I feel,' says Neville, doubtfully.

'Well, what you think?' shouts Kitty, 'They start

building something new and different? Take what there is. 'Renounce, appropriate. Burn the past,' that's what you do.'

'I guess that could be justice,' Alvin says.

'I don't know what it is,' says Kitty.

'That's you,' Regina says, fired up by some response. 'That's Kitty, that's the stereotype. Your bum settled hard on someone else's chintz.'

'And stereotype yourself,' says Kitty, making a fist.

'I dare say we're all stereotypes,' says Alvin, soothing. 'Each in their own particular way.'

The burn goes on. Our bunch – we're interested in the economics, shipping out. Here, instead, it must be religion, factions, clans.

'No, no,' says Neville. 'It's the beginning of the end, for sure. Like Paola says. That's why she stays at home – she's such a drag with portents and the like.'

'We shall slim down, is all,' says Alvin. 'Agree. No rancour, just like the five of us.'

'This ship – could be a space ship, in a movie. Escaping the end, the sacrifice. Except it's cramped,' I say.

'That would be the budget,' Alvin says, as if he knows.

The smoke's now black. 'There go your cushions, Kitty,' says Regina, with some malice.

'If we're a space ship, or we're just a ship, we cannot flee, nor fly,' says Kitty, 'So, we need a captain.'

'Yes, that's it!' Regina shouts. 'The third estate – it's everything. Then we cop out, elect some guy that tells us what to do. That's your democracy! Kitty – you're a dope, a boss's gal!' There's much confabulation. In the end, I'm the captain, the one they hate the most, the one who didn't want the job.

'We can't live like animals, in a pack, like cards,' says Neville. 'Bossed by some ancient guy who screws the women.'

'These religious wars,' says Alvin. 'The chiliasts – they are the best. They give you something to expect, to wait for.'

'That's not the whole,' says Neville. 'Big interests. Past and future, it is all in play.'

'Sure, everything is part of everything,' says Alvin, irritated. 'But – if there's no conclusions, you can't have new starts.'

'Look!' says Kitty. 'Fireworks.'

So there are: rejoice. Conclusion. There's tracks of phosphorus, then golden hail, squirrels blue and red, flowers that boil and run. Then bang bang BANG. It ends.

'Maybe modernity has come,' I say. 'New life! Free! And not. It's quite complex. At least there's shopping.'

'Shipping too,' laughs Neville.

Then they turn on me:

'Of course,' says Alvin. 'You're not qualified.'

'We're still stuck here,' Regina says.

'I know,' I say. 'I don't believe. No gods, no emperors, no heroes – that's my creed. Raise the black flag…' and I go on. They are not satisfied. Indeed, my discourse angers them.

The captain, the real captain, comes on board. 'I'll land you on the shore,' he says.

'No, no,' we shout, but it's no use, and on the shore we go.

Some angry guys show up, they take us into jail. A loose environment, it seems – there's people shuffled in and out, and stories long as books, some torture, some cut deals. A guy says, 'You're safer here, than where the guys outside are settling scores.'

No doubt it's true – but we were better still upon our boat. 'This certainly is "after", but there's consequences you like, and those that simply come along,' I say. Each moment here's a capsule holding lives that sprout and burst – a blink, and we have victory, defeat. Another – here's the revolution and its counter. Another blink – we're freed from jail, 'Before we figure out what you've done wrong,' they say.

'Somewhere there'll be a bar that's selling,' Kitty says.

There's guys with turtles on a stall.

'Let's free some too,' Regina says.

'No,' I say. 'Effi needs them by the hundred,' and they stare at me.

'I'm quite converted,' Alvin says. 'They'll need a guy like me. There's my cash, too ...'

Regina seems put out. 'I've always been a revolutionary,' she says. 'But then the politics gets in – you see it here, you see the black holes open up ...'

'It's the adrenalin, Regina,' Alvin says. 'You get the

same effect from jumping off a bridge. The trouble is, my love, you're superficial. Try working in the factory I'll bring—'

'We're overtired,' says Neville. 'Our benevolence, wanting to do the good – it's coming to an end. The storm has passed, we need to break the spell.' I'd like to leave: it's like passing through the market, seeing the stomach work, the digestion. Best not linger. Kitty has found her bottle. Maybe in a while she'll dance. Alvin says to some guys hanging round – 'I'll be bringing work and cash. I know you'll keep it safe.' The guys grin. It says 'Harvard' on their shirts. 'Yes,' Neville says. 'It'll all start up again. It must. I'll be here. I told you I was for the revolution.'

'I should leave,' I tell them.

'Don't wave your black flag too much, my friend,' says Alvin. 'People don't like you if you're not enthusiastic for new orders.'

'I know,' I say.

'You think only of yourself, the immediate fragments of perception, colliding with your consciousness,' says Neville.

'I know just what you mean, Neville,' I say. 'But I don't think you've said it right, what you've just said.'

'He means you!' says Kitty. 'You can't piece a scene together, make it whole, make it part of a panorama. You're too small, I guess. Low down.'

'You don't like me, that's all it is,' I say. 'That's quite ok. It's not obligatory to like.'

'You see!' says Alvin. 'Here, it's history. You – it's

always you. It's individualism run wild. You're like a beast that has no history, no tradition. And the values that come with.'

'Well, sure, I don't let those things out, to show,' I say, doubtfully.

Regina isn't here. 'She's letting guys convince her they are doing right,' says Neville. 'She gets taken in too deep. She respects – unlike you. But then – I have to pull her out.'

There's no sign of her. Guys in big cars drive up and down the shuttered street: they shout and sing.

The three walk away from me.

I go back to the jail. The guy's not pleased to see me. 'Hey!' I say. 'Those two guys and the tipsy lady – maybe you let them go too soon. You know, for them, it's profit that they see in all this sacrifice. Starting up their digging, and their scams. Corruption, too, I bet.'

I hang around. A big car takes the three, my friends, back to the jail, and then inside.

Somewhere outside, Regina's free. She'll never know who gave the gift, her freedom. Maybe she wouldn't understand. She'll seek out Neville – or she won't. Not to have him – it's a sacrifice. So is to have him. The fighting here – is it the beginning of the end, or a part of it? I'd need to ask Regina. Maybe there's an end to her and Neville too, with him in jail. Perhaps she'll wonder where he is ...

I've finished here. I go back to see Paola. Remember not to talk of them, Neville, Regina.

Paola's lying on a mattress. How white it is in here. How white she is. She says, 'You see, I am depressed. I'm like the Snow Queen, waiting for my prince. A special kiss.'

'You've got the story wrong,' I say. 'But you have what I always wanted – remember what the song says, "A white room, without curtains". And you understand, the white light coming in, uninterrupted, forceful. And you, Paola, lying there, your skin so white, the little scoops of breast, so white, so kissable.'

'Yes, yes,' she says. 'The sacrifice. The end. How it depresses us. Come, lie beside me, and let me see a landscape on these walls. The trees – they should be indigo, the sand – is red as garnets, the sea is maybe grey, or green?' And she turns to me, and asks, her mouth is close, the lips are red as garnets and the breath – grey-green as aloes. 'Grey? Or green?' she asks. 'The sea?'

There is a rule – you mustn't fall into the sea, you mustn't fall into the grey and green depression Paola has – and as she asks, she pulls herself a little higher, and her breasts are bare, she says,

'They tell me I have lovely breasts,' and I say,

'Who are these "they"? Is there some contest you have won, dear Paola? That would not be a surprise ...' and on I talk, because I know three things, like in the fairy tales; not mention Neville, not drop Regina's name. And not involve myself with people who're depressed, they're in a magic web that sucks you in, they pass it on, the malady, the charm. Depression, it's a spell, and maybe you can break it, by doing what you mustn't do, taking her and sharing it, and lying on a bed somewhere and waiting for the prince, or the princess, after a hundred depressing years, that you can ask to paint the landscape on the white wall where the light hits with all its force ...

'No, no, Paola, really – I've no libido left,' I say – but it's too late. I do exactly what I should not do. She lies, a white ermine curling on the mattress – and at last her eyes are open, and they're blue, sea blue. 'I waited here,' she says, 'So long, until my depression could be passed on. The sacrifice, the species' end – it's all passed on, it's disappeared.'

'I know all about that,' I say. 'The sacrifice, the end. It isn't malady. It's an hypothesis.'

'Fuck you!' she shouts. 'You know it's happening. You've tramped the world. You know!'

'Yes, Paola. Yes, I know,' I say.

There's something bounding up the stairs. Jump, jump, it goes. It comes in on us – a beast with sporgent eyes, a black mask on the white, a lemur.

'Here,' says Paola. 'This guy, this lemma ... See his legs – the back ones are so long, he can't bend down, go on all fours, he has to jump. Look at the eyes, so sad, they know about extinction, you can see. Take him – take him back to Effi. He's taken my depression, taken it off you too, and bears it all himself.'

It could be so. He's miserable for sure, and we – Paola and me – we're feeling good.

I travel with the lemur.

There's the Bir-Hakeim bridge, the trains.

'Effi, who's the guy who left? I passed him on the stair.' I ask.

'Oh, just a guy I owed,' she says.

'Neville's no more with us, Effi, I'm afraid,' I say. 'There was a battle. Maybe a decisive one. Then he got in wrong with the new guys. He wanted everything to carry on, to stay the same, to go back like it was. We'll need another agent.'

She seems distracted, so I say, 'I brought a lemur. Some people say it's called a "lemma".'

'No, no,' she says. 'They got it wrong. A lemma's quite another thing. I'll call it "Lemmy". Like the movie guy, "*les données immédiates* ..."' It fits animals. You must remember Alphaville?'

We hear it jumping up and down the stairs. Depressed.

'What shall we do with it?' I ask.

'Something will come to us,' she says. 'It always does. Though why you brought just one, I cannot think. Anyway, you're safe here for a bit. Don't think about the animal. It won't be around for long.'

'Well,' I say, annoyed. 'What I have seen – the battle, justice being done, all that – if it means something, as it must, then single creatures must mean something too. A couple, or a troop, is quite another thing. My search took all my qualities. They say they're ghosts: those creatures last for ever.'

She's not convinced.

She says, 'I guess it could be worth a lot. If anybody still collects exotic things.'

THE GUARDIANS

Work? No work. You can sit at home, or walk, and face rejection, refusal, in person.

I walk; that way your singing gets a rhythm. Down here, there's modern stuff tacked on. There's clubs, and pubs. You're always looking, for it, work. You don't want what you'd get. Down here, down south, it's always been a torment, work. There's a smell of Africa. Magna Grecia – Greeks long gone, left some scrap of dialect. The people here are dark, dark as goths. Chalky faces, Arab faces, Norman hair; a spatter of occupations left, the military ones, with lords in castles. Stony fields and figs. Albanians and tarantellas. Aren't those Slovak gypsies? – hated there, hated, ignored, here. What's the difference for them? Settlement – a drag, a bitch. Walking – the scene is always changing, and you remain the same.

Some guy says to me, 'You look free. Empty. How's about a day of watching nature, well concealed?'

Why not. I'm quite drunk. Anything will do, so long as it's tomorrow.

'They cross here,' says Dex. 'People, animals. It's a march, a confine, that we're in. This is a route, for migration.' We're pressed up close. In the hide, we've waited hours to see those two birds screw. Sex. Was it for this they built the Eiffel Tower?

Dex says, 'You'd better not talk. It gives you away.'

You like to know the country you're in, the side you're on.

The hide is best cover. I whisper, 'I hone my brain on games. It isn't fun, unless you like snuff movies. Someone you'll never see must have won, some time. There's oriental mumble in there – reach the highest level, see how top clever you are, but – aha! – I got there before you, wrote the finale long before. You start from the bottom, reach the determined end, if you're that smart. Is that Buddhism, then? Some guy has scripted it, from California, so "the struggle naught availeth".'

'Of course, struggles avail. Games, too. Even this, the wait, is a struggle,' Dex says. We're awfully close together, here in this hide.

At the end, you know what every animal knows, you go out alone. The herd moves on. Better for you, that you leave no consciousness behind. It's cancelled out, the emotions, the stage, are needed for someone else. I say,

'This old guy – long ago, a time of death squads ... his comrades disappeared, he was cast up, whittled away, on the tundra, on the ice. And he survived, and as he lived, he felt an anguish you can't imagine.'

Dex doesn't speak, he hushes: I go on, 'Things re-compose. There'll be someone there to feed the starving ... these postcolonial wars – slaughterings in silence. The religions, with their flags – must be something underneath, besides, they're quite unreadable. Unimaginable, that people fight for the unknowable. It must be the taste. But – this old guy, it wasn't guilt he felt, but impotence. No one understood, because he had an easy life. "Good for him", with malice, that's what they said.' Dex says,

'It seems to me irrelevant, all this. They screamed, the lucky ones who had the moment when they knew it all. They died. And he went on, your guy, tolerated in his indifferent place, well paid. So what? If all he wanted was a recognition of his misery ...'

There's no such thing as coming to terms. There's forgetting. I say,

'Every idea has terrible consequences. The more you have, and sharper, the more guys look up to you, try to explain why things went wrong. Justice, benevolence, end in massacres. If you're just the executioner, you're looked down upon.'

Dex says, 'I like the story of the lead guitarist – his mates gave him a double dose of his drugs, left him unconscious in the men's room, stole his money and documents ... He understood. They didn't want him in the band.' I say,

'I didn't know there was a lead anything. I didn't think they listened to one another. That's why they keep splitting up.' Dex says, almost in silence,

'Here, we can see anything that walks or flies. You know, we bird people, we do terrible things. These birds here –' and there they are, like silver storks on a kimono – 'They used to be monogamous, roamed, always returned, to just the one place, home. We introduced them to adultery. Then free for all. And turned their gyroscopes around. They flew all which way. Maybe they'd known distances, and times – not the landscapes, which we changed. Everyone changed the landscape – they always have. The birds had fits!' He laughs.

Why are we here? Are we for the good? Are we for the bad? Or bits of both.

'I'm Cajun,' Dex says, 'We say "Acajyàn", people think we're saying "a Canadian". Ignorant. No geography.'

A string of tall black men lopes by. 'Count them, count them,' whispers Dex.

'Why?' I whisper.

'Just count them. If you don't count them, who will? The State?' he laughs. 'The cops are after them to send them back. They're from Senegal – you can tell, by the shape of their ouds. They'll wish they hadn't got the jobs they get.'

The birds don't seem in the mood for sex. You can see two villages, churches with umber cottages around in hope. 'Whose territory is this?' I ask.

'The left belongs to the Frattali. The right – the Prestaletti. In between is no man's land. Nothing. No one. No traffic, no trade.'

Two wolves, or something like, go by: 'Don't count those,' says Dex. 'It ends bad for them, if there's too many.'

'It's an art,' I say. 'This counting. Where it all ends up.'

'That's not your concern,' says Dex. 'Counting is an end. Then there are other ends. You must have known that.

In the bar, when you asked me for a job – you must already know the numbers are applied to everything that walks or flies.'

'I know I was drunk. I know I have no money,' I say.

'Exactly. Two kinds of knowing,' says Dex.

Was I a pickup? Is he gay, a killer? Or need help.

'*Je ne suis pas ton ennemi,*' I say, to cheer him: it comes from a movie.

'These birds,' he says. 'Used to live up high. Now, it's bushes. And they're happy to have two good-looking guys like us to watch. You know,' he presses closer. 'They used to think they brought the babies. Now, we watch them having theirs. It's the great turn, the turnaround. The Indians used to bring them back, the dead,' and he blows into his hands. 'It worked when there were few of them.'

No one is dead here. I remember the Indian gesture, from a movie.

'People,' he says. 'Want reassurance. But – it must be from someone that they trust. The commonplaces – they must come from pretty lips. A dodgy guy, like you or me – they wouldn't listen. It has to be a prophet or a whitecoat, that says "the end is nigh". Not you. Or me.'

He's talking loudly now. The birds seem used to that. 'The trouble is,' he says. 'That you are full of sentiment. Empty of all the rest. "Poor people", as they run; you say "poor animals", as they stare back. "Death is all around", you say, "I'll replace it with my empathy, that I'll call love." My trouble is the opposite of yours. If we are watching death, then it is so. And we shall watch. If there's advantage, I shall take it. My tears – are tears for me. Reserved. And not much use.'

How we sweat, here in this hide, this box. It's grave sweat, of what we've eaten long ago.

Dex says, 'It doesn't bother me – a guy, he wants to build a house,' and he points to a purple blank in the dip. 'Or take some pills, and sell them to his mates. The trouble is – it's power that counts, not pills or permits. The clever ones, they have the power. They sell and they connive. My trouble is – I'm too intelligent. They know if I come in, I'd need to be the boss. Intelligence, and power. If you're bright, you have to turn it into power. That makes you vulnerable. They do for you,' and he sighs. 'Your mates. They off you, in a flash. So I'm on the other side. At least, I'm in between. But you,' he turns to me. 'You're just a drunk. No one will roll you – you're no fun. You're a clock. Time passes on your face.'

'No, no,' I say. 'I'm just a standard pilgrim. Beat with my stave, and sing along, the chant ...'

The reek of our sweat – what can we have eaten, through our lives? – reaches the birds, and they lift off. Dex says,

'Protect and threaten, that's the way with birds, and guys. You think you protect those storks. We are not armed – but if we were....that way you can defend yourself, the world. With guys, it is the same: you threaten, then you give protection. Everything is all the same. It's nature, and you need to have it, all around.'

He presses his moist beaky face up close, as if he

wants to show inside his nose: 'People like sex, or say they do,' he says. 'They make great efforts over it, although it brings them grief. Look at the birds, and how they suffer. Just one poke. And then – those goddam eggs, the scarlet throats, the squeaky squawks. The irresistible, the suicidal, drive. The impulse. Keep yourself far from that, my friend. Remember our motto – "Threaten and protect". That's all you need.'

His breath – it's like wet rats. He says, 'Today we threaten wolves, protect the storks. Tomorrow – it's the wolves that get protection. Don't you want to be the one that orders that?'

'Dex,' I say. 'There's not much here. Just sitting in a bush. You want to be a crime boss – but your fear, intelligence – it holds you back. Perhaps you're quite like me – but different ...'

We pack the hide away.

'That's the work,' says Dex. 'That's what it is.'

We're in the bar again, we drink my pay: 'That's what nature earns for you,' he says.

I say, 'How strange we are, they surely think. Shooting, trapping, gutting them. Healing and counting them.'

'You talking about animals now?' asks Dex. 'You really can do sentiment! Animals, people – it's all the same to you! Your tears will fall, quite indiscriminate, and salt your steak ...'

'That's cheap, Dex,' I say. 'They didn't pay enough for meat ...'

'"They" didn't pay anything,' says Dex. 'I paid. I want you to work with me.'

'There is no work,' I say.

'Yesterday we did none. But my ambition – there it lay, you saw it – a carpet over no man's land,' he says.

'My path,' I say. 'Does not end here. Maybe, in Africa ...'

'Oh yes,' says Dex. 'You have the calling. That I see. I need you here, however, for a task. My fear – is not of death, of suffering no more. It's what they do to you before. And then – suppose they make you disappear, dissolved in acid, as if you'd never been? No stone, no name, no epitaph, to keep your spirit safely underground. Your thoughts, your poetry, authority – your lymph ... your sperm – all bubbled up in toxic smoke. No, my dear friend – I'll smooth your path when it is time to go. A peddlar's pack of cash for you to take; I'll cut new staves, compose bright chants ... And – like they say – a mission statement too. But now, I have some work for you.'

'Dex, please!' I say. 'We watched the birds. They do what all birds do. The wolves will get them, if they're nesting on the floor. We have no pressing interest there, for one or other kind ...'

'No, no!' Dex shouts. 'Forget the birds. You have to dig a hole for me, a hiding place. Beneath the landscape, where I hide, and give my orders from. So, I'll be safe. A bunker. Shelter. *Mon repos.*'

I have no choice. I'm unemployed, can't plumb or wire, or anything. We bathe the pact in booze. My destiny, it seems, is just what comes along, there's no way back. I have to dig his hole, alone, to keep it secret – then ... will he kill me with my spade, and bury me, and stopper up the deed?

'Have no fear,' says Dex. 'Danger is around, but first for me, not you.'

'Enterprise is a good,' I say. 'The guys need jobs.'

'Spreading happiness,' says Dex. 'Is a good. A duty, even. Pills, permits and *putes*.'

'Hedonism is what we're after,' I say. 'But you'll sit terrified, down in your hole. It's all set up for others – love, desire. You just get cash that you can't spend.'

He's annoyed: he says, 'But you! You – you're just the guy with the shovel.'

It's true. I look at the truth like it was a movie of me – doubled up and picking strawberries. Or further on, down South some more, shovelling in a sulphur mine.

'It's not just digging. You could build a city here. It would be splendid, and I'd be the boss,' Dex says.

'What would all the people do?' I ask. He's expansive.

'In China, they've got socialism, with capitalists. Here, there's cops and judges, doctors, senators – then there's the mafias. Those Chinese – they'll have to watch themselves. The capitalists. They'll do all the work,' says Dex.

'When you have dug the hole,' he says. 'You're free to go. But if you want, I'll show a way for you to take. I'll show you what's your destiny.'

Fun City. Crime City. A stork on every chimney. Tall palaces, all replicas of something else.

'You might go into politics,' I tell Dex, greasing him along.

'I *am* in politics,' he says. 'It's not the votes that count, it is the show you must put on. There's women that'll do that for you. The smell of power – for them, it's like the smell of sweat. It is their destiny, it pulls them, like a rope.'

Dex is a bit of Indian, of Yankee, maybe Cajun too, just like he says – a kind of onion of ethnicities. I could flatten him, upon his soil, the birds will have his eyes, the wolves enjoy his testicles, the bushes hide the flaccid rest, the bristly gristle, long white thighs. But – what would be in it for myself? Where is the profit?

'I'm the prophet, I'm the messenger,' he says. He doesn't touch his drink, so I have his, and mine as well. 'You are the revelation, you're the wanderer. I'm the builder, and I show the guys how they should realise their fantasies. And you're the fall guy, on his quest, promising and conning. Fuck all, is what you get. Illusion's what you'll leave behind; and picking cucumbers – that's what you'll do.'

'Look, Dex,' I say. 'There's a woman, here in the bar. She's loose. Enough for two.' There's always one in bars like this, a pebble in a centrifuge, you know it ends in breaking glass.

'No, no,' he says. 'I don't go for ladies. It's my thing. Their little hands, around your secrets. It's enough to know they'll give you anything they've got, so as to get some back. The rest is – shots in the dark, my friend.'

The lady's – not a dog, at least. She's full of lore and stories – comes from a village nearby Košice. 'Oh yes, the railway line,' I say. 'When I had cash, I roamed round there. The horses pulling strings of lowdown carts, the song, the dance ...'

'That must be long ago, that you had cash! No horses now ... It wasn't always so,' she says. 'That was the Lithuanian empire, once. Before I got there,' and she laughs. 'If you were there, why don't you write a book? On living rough, and walking. Remembering how it was. Maybe you sometimes took the train to Košice, like me.'

'What kind of book?' I ask. 'The one that says, "Be humble. Love the next guy – he may give you work. Don't steal small change – it's capital you need. If you don't find it, love makes do?"'

She's quite amazed, she stares at me: 'Why yes!' she says. 'You are a kind of genius. A book like that makes stacks of cash.'

'A movie makes lots more,' says Dex.

'Oh no,' she – Mavra – says, 'I don't do sex. Not with some guy that's on the road,' and she's clutching Dex's arm as if it were a leg: 'It's just my thing. Not personal. I'm not into videos.'

*

I dig out his refuge. I'm used to this. He says, 'Incredible.

Astounding. So quick, I don't have the cash to pay you.'

'I don't want it,' I say. 'Money binds. Just a few rounds – then I'll be off. The mission!'

We three – the bar; we sit, our voices rise like steam. 'Storks,' says Dex. 'And cane toads.'

'Frogs,' says Mavra. 'You want the guys to watch and learn from nature. You must elect a boss. The frogs choose storks, and are consumed. They'd done nothing wrong.'

'The people understand, and learn. A little army too, is what you need. Some drones. Some stuff that lets you see at night,' says Dex.

'Oh no,' says Mavra. 'I'm not into this, the marching up and down, the shouts. I had that all at home,' and there are tears, she turns and clings to me, and things pour out, the loss of what she's had, the loss of what she didn't have. She often cries, the tears are similar, they don't avail.

'Courage, Mavra, you never quite have anything,' I say. 'It's always slippery, what you've got.'

'And war,' says Dex. 'We'll live with that. It shakes the tiny bits of glass in the kaleidoscope. It jumbles up, and moves along. It's the defence of what you've got and wanting more – especially obedience. You two – I guess you've got some lack, you're patsies! I'm the normal guy, and normal guys will live and work where I shall build.'

'I'd not build my city there, on the plain,' says Mavra. 'I'd want one on a hill, just like they say. With trains. I'm not so sure about having people, though.'

'You can dig in, and there's water for the frogs. The

toads,' Dex says.

'There's layers of earlier cities, under the scrub,' I say.

Already you can hear the frogs, they're croaking 'fuckit fuckit fuckit'.

'It's the food chain,' Dex says. 'We're in it too. The Greeks wrote plays about it.'

'Stay with me, stay with me,' says Mavra to me, crying again. 'Don't leave, not ever.'

'What can you do for me, Mavra,' I ask, 'except weigh down?'

'Don't ask that,' Mavra shouts. 'Other people are always useful, sometimes. Besides, I talk funny, surely you hear that? They'd send me to the Funny Factory. It's obsessive, what they do, and what they make. It's where the bright kids go, it calms them down. When you speak in your own way, so, they diagnose. It ends up – that you're working class.'

'It's that you're Slovak, Mavra. Besides, in Crime City, there'll be minorities. You can't speak against that,' I say.

'No, no,' she shouts, so loud, that I'm embarrassed for Dex – 'I don't want to live there, not with him in a burrow, like the worm that flies in the night. Into our secret pockets.'

'I don't want followers,' I say. 'They slow you down. Nor precursors – they make you sweat.'

'I'm not stupid,' Mavra says fiercely. 'I was at school. We read Proust, all one day. I have a view on life, and all the people round. The fops, the invalids, the doormen, bankers, and the sensitives. I'm complex, too. How can you know what justice is, for me? You can't even speak one language that we speak at home.'

'I can't give you justice, Mavra,' I say. 'I doubt that anyone is able to, or even grasp what it might mean. And – people are less complex now, you understand. They're not so interesting, don't mix together like they used. They stay away as much they can from one another, if the other seems the freaky sort.'

I missed that day at school, it seems, when they did Proust.

Mavra says she'll do her courtship dance, then we'll decide who stays with her. Dex gives her coldeye, says, 'That's good for storks, maybe ...' but she is whirling round, like the bottle on the table-top that spins for truth or forfeit – and for sure, there's breakages as you'd expect, it's those long stick legs of hers ... Dex shouts, 'Look! You and your Proust! What have you done ...?'

The guy behind the bar ushers us out, Mavra and me, he says, 'No gypsies here,' but quiet – a rule, and not an insult.

So we go.

'Dex isn't bad, not evil,' Mavra says. 'Those palaces – when they fall on you, they do no harm. Just made of sifted sand, like castor sugar. He has his utopia, all the guys stand equal. Himself, the guiding principle. Not just a boss. A boss of all the bosses, wiping out their pettiness, overlaying their ambition. Then, there's the sanctuary. The marsh. The swamp. The bog, the slough. His nature.'

'Good, Mavra!' I tell her. 'That's how we spread the word, that's what he told us to. But he won't pay us for it, as what we do is quite incalculable. His vision is our destiny – it won't translate to cash. The earning and the eating, all the rest, the good and bad that comes from him – we have no part in that.'

Here we are, on the road again. 'What can you do for me, Mavra?' I ask. 'I'm a marvel with my shovel, but it doesn't pay.'

'Oh,' she laughs, 'I can wash and bury you, like I did to my father, mean old sod. I told you, on the road, I don't do sex. Besides – look at the *putes*! There's lots, and young and pretty too.'

Maybe she killed her father, and that's why ...

Maybe both of us were born to live in Dex's city: Crime City. Open a stall. Sell goldfish, something like, the mouths they open constantly, and not a word comes out. That's what you need. Silence and gold.

'Don't look back,' says Mavra. 'The city's taking on its form. We might want to live there.'

We turn and look. In the midst of the purple up rise the buildings of white sand ... bowls, billows, water mirrors that reflect the heights and lay them calmly flat. Pediments and perrons. A city fit for angels.

'Hear the surf!' says Mavra. 'The sand in the cement. The grinding of the molluscs, their shells, the bones of hammerheads, blue whales, their songs ethereal.'

'Will Dex rule the world from here?' I ask. His city –

how impressive. Himself safe, beneath.

'Maybe he already does,' says Mavra. 'Him and his mates.'

'We'll need to learn some French,' I say. 'That's not so bad.'

'You're not Rom,' Mavra says.

'There's no class in telling the bar guy that,' I say. 'What's the difference anyway?'

'You're in danger, now,' says Mavra. 'You know all his secrets, where he's buried, who he'll do alliances with.'

'He let me go,' I say.

'"One day" he said he'd let you go ...' she says.

I don't see her for some time. Then – she's been tattooed, a beard, a blue imperial, on her chin.

'No good,' I say. 'Mavra, I still recognise you.'

'No, no,' she says. 'It's not disguise – it's my "keep off" sign.'

'It's good you're hopeful, Mavra. If Dex wants, he'll seek us out,' I say, 'Alas, you're still you, and I still look like me.'

'Dex respects you greatly,' Mavra says.

Too much Proust – has gone to her chin. 'I want to meet all kinds,' she says. 'All the characters.'

There's not much to say to that. The characters – they do no harm.

The modern city, down there in the dip: in the sun, it seems a mirage, just *plastiques*. Only the storks and frogs persist. They're real, quite primitive. She says,

'Dex thinks you're a pure soul, an idiot. No money, sex, position: all renounced. On his own, he can't think further than his orders, and his fears. He says you have the vision. A sequence of development. Beyond the storks and frogs, a time may come with no more thugs, enforcers. That is all he knows, but you see something more. Not the villagers around, the guys, potatoes in the sack – but great potential. Love? Equality? Who knows. It's quite exciting!'

And it is! Her strange face, its decoration – comes at me, as if it's from an island, from some space. 'I'm scared,' I say. 'If you're caught out, Dex can be sharp. Sharp like a scythe.'

'So long as he's behind us, and we're running on,' she says, 'it's as it all should be. It's when he bars the road ...'

'You've messed yourself up,' Dex says to Mavra. 'What can you do now?'

'Well,' she says, 'I've no choice but to follow him,' and she points at me. 'And so he's no choice but to lead me somewhere.'

'What can you do, Mavra?' asks Dex, irritated.

'I can wash the dead,' she says.

'OK!' says Dex. 'That's one thing we need. But I need this guy,' and he hugs me. 'To build my city. The model – you've imagined it ... Now, execution!'

'I'll need some help.' I say. 'With sea-sandy concrete, on a marsh – it'll crumble, or it sinks.'

'Yes, yes,' shouts Dex. 'That's exactly it! Acceleration! Stimulus! Let it crumble, let it sink, in foxtrot time. We'll truck new people in, and new materials, and new ideas. Faster and faster, it must revolve. The thing is to keep the frogs and storks. They are our reference.'

'We withdrew,' I say, proudly. 'Mavra and I. To contemplate. We found a stillness. Nothing doing. No flow of cash.'

'That's crap,' says Dex. 'Withdrawing, thinking you can have it all. That's the temptation – your mind is blank, and you mistake the emptiness for revelation, for the sum. It is not so. Down on the plain, the storks are bringing babies in, our population is taking off. As we grow rich, so we defraud. We seem an affluent stillness, but we're circular. We profit, and we skim. We make the stuff that other guys invent, and steal the plans for different stuff. We copy and we innovate. There's shootouts and there's hospitals. There's war and peace. Your vision – needs the palaces to fit it in, that's all. It's frogs and storks – a symbiosis. Just don't bring in more predators. You'll need to love the frogs, and their abounding libido, their lust for life ... hallucinogenic skins.'

'The towers that I'll build for you – they'll all fall down,' I say, not knowing where that leads.

'That's why I'm underground,' says Dex. 'Although it's damp. Of course they'll fall, the towers, and other guys will stand them up, and skim their riches from the crap they'll make them of. In Cajun, "*exploit*" means achievement, but you sentimental guys! – the stuff that you buy cheap, it comes from guys who're only paid enough to keep them coming in, day after day, and making it.. They're here at first, and then they're over there and out of sight. All cities are like this – they're built on crime and indolence, and guys complaining at their lot. That's why there's storks and frogs – I brought them here in order to instruct, not to pretend they're beautiful.'

Later, Mavra says to me, 'The trouble is, Dex is a philosopher, and you are not. You never had a trade. The money that you took – it's gone, you're just another raft at sea. Your flaccid sails would fill with good intentions, but there's flat calm. You paddle, or you don't, to reach that slippery grey rock, its sides are glassy sheer.'

'I'm not humble, Mavra. I don't need to know my place,' I say. 'The answer is – more predators. I've dug for Dex. Now, to stir him up ... More predators! Different ones.'

Is the city built, or is it the future we don't want to spoil?

'Dex has all the money for it, down in his hole. It is as good as built,' says Mavra. 'Even better. All our problems will be solved, when it's in real time. I don't have problems now, myself, but when it's up, I'll have them, someone will resolve them all.'

An answer's with the animals. Cats? Monkeys? Sharks?

'The city's built,' says Dex, packing money into bags.

'It's only in your heads,' says Mavra. We ignore this.

'Here's a contract,' Dex tells me, waving some calligraphy.

'No, no,' I say. 'I'm not for killing guys that give you stares.'

'You have to spin the tale,' says Dex, ignoring me. 'I've settled nature – now I have to get some guys who'll do the work on all the rest.'

'They can't be locals,' Mavra says. 'So, they must be Chinese.'

They build a club. They're Chinese – quite the wrong sort. They drink, they gamble, and they sing. There's boxing, and there's food all day.

'They're eating all the frogs,' Dex says. 'Maybe they'll eat the storks, and then we'll have no births. Well, maybe that's quite good – there's nowhere they can sleep...'

'Look, Dex,' I say. 'Don't take it seriously. We know that on this marsh a city can be built and sink, there'll be malaria and clots of cars around. We have the cash. I have the vision. Our destiny's revealed, we can't retouch it, and those Chinese – we'll brush them from our minds, and all will be restored to pristine pools and bog.'

'You two,' says Mavra. 'Don't understand your trade. If you don't build, more money will come in. Dex will be rich as India. Guys will come in, they speculate on voids, not finished stuff. They give you cash. Nature's nearly virginal, the value is preserved, it grows – and we are not disturbed. No one to pay for doing stressful work, no one inventing jobs to do. No cops. Just frogs and storks.'

She's right. As well as Proust, she must read Capital. Another day at school I missed.

We summon up the Chinese crew. Quite the wrong sort, they are. In the flesh, and in their shed – they roister. My! They're hard! They never spare themselves, they box and game, they take the pills Dex sells. They bring their *putes* – so beautiful, so hard, and such long hair ...

'And of course,' says Mavra, 'the message this guy brings,' and she joins her hands before me – '"all is love, forgiveness, second lives" – all that can be stored up against the day we're all sucked down.'

All this is true. The problem is – the Chinese eat the frogs. I'm unemployed again. My mission statement's stoppered up in scrolls.

'You're useless here,' says Dex to both of us. 'Now I am rich, I'll send you off, to seek a thing for me, and maybe you'll get rich as well. I'll send two hard Chinese guys with you – they've lost at cards, and they don't box. They're finished now. Here's Mister Han. And Mister Wu.'

All over, there are schemes – to turn a country into something fresh – all sugar cane, all butterflies, windmills, martial arts. We shall describe the plan, and take the cash. Guys are impressed, they pay. And we move on. And Han and Wu protect our backs.

Mister Han says, 'It seems an ordinary kind of scam,' and Mister Wu says, 'We'll run fast – not the sun, but danger's at our backs.'

'What is the "thing" you want us to bring back?' asks Mavra. 'We'll need excuses, if we find it isn't there.'

Dex says, 'The storks, the frogs – they go so far, and

then they stop. It is instructive – so are Proust and Marx. But – I want something more – that breaks the chain of eat-be eaten.'

'Something vegetarian?' Mister Han suggests.

'Some hybrid – not too strange, but multifaceted. That walks and swims and flies. Maybe a picture of it does as well,' says Mister Wu, who paints and draws.

'We could get one made, for sure,' says Mister Han. 'Not being delicate about it – what you find, walking in the fields, and what you make to order, mostly what's involved is time. The making cuts it short.'

We look over the swamp to where the shepherds sit, and spy on one another. 'Those guys that Dex puts in the bogs,' says Mister Wu. 'They're trussed like goats, the wire goes round their ankles to their throat. When they're dug up, they'll think it was a ritual.'

'Of course it was,' says Mavra. 'No religion, and no politics. Just values kicking in.'

'It's quiet and quick, an easy way,' says Mister Han. 'If you don't struggle, and just let it come. Besides, if there's some guy betrays you, gives the coldeye – what can you do? He's useless ...'

'People should communicate,' says Mavra. 'That way you can tell them no. Or maybe yes. What you don't want is what Dex calls the *coup de foudre*. Trussed up and pleading, like a hen.'

'It could be just a matter of the categories,' I say. 'When Adam named the animals, for sure he left some out. We find one of the nameless ones – that is the sample that

Dex wants. Instructive – perhaps too of a beauty unsurpassable. Or cunning. Able to use tools, or count, or change its colour. Or its skin.'

We look at Mavra's face; its overwhelming blue suggests a track, a piece of evidence.

'What we should do,' says Mister Wu, 'is find out what Dex wants, and then we'll find it for him.'

'Maybe it's love,' laughs Mister Han.

'Your friend Dex,' says Mister Wu, 'is rubbish. It's not about nice things at all.'

I say, 'Let's think – what does he want? A creature that swims and flies and walks?' I'm defeated.

'A duck,' says Mavra.

'Or at least a swan,' says Mister Wu.

Dex has an entrepôt. All around is Italy. It looks quite like these villages. Dex's place is special, but it's much the same as all around. No country in particular, yet unmistakable.

'All over,' Mavra says. 'There's tattooed people. A mark of nobility, maybe sacredness.'

'If everybody has them, they are nothing,' says Mister Han. 'It's just an ugliness you wrongly think's magnificent.'

'Maybe it is,' says Mavra, irritated. 'It sets me quite apart. And if it comes from Proust – it's all about dead ancestors, mostly destroyed, and mostly gay.'

'Come on,' I say. 'What creature can it be? A lunar animal? A jaguar.'

'In any case, a waste to hunt for it, then gift it on to

Dex,' says Mister Wu.

What a fine couple they are, he and Mister Han. Strange, that they're so bad at cards.

I say, 'A spider? Like a queen? A fish, an abalone? A bird mask ...' and then I realise – 'A person. In a bird mask. Doing the black things Dex no doubt dreams of.'

'Of course! – a person,' Mavra says. 'That must be the answer. There's lots can swim and walk. But – flies?'

'We didn't come by train, you know,' says Mister Wu, quite sharp: 'We flew. Three abilities – a super potent beast. It's like three tricky things you'll find in Dex – coca, capital – and *conneries*.'

'Dex doesn't trust the humans,' Mavra says. 'Why should he want to meet this person? Guy from some cartel? A banker? Who can tell?'

People are impressed by these Chinese. We must be serious, they think, with easy pickings for them, credit going back and based on gold, and schemes that make the value swell like a balloon – the land, location, – you don't even need to dig.

'My, this scam's banal,' says Mavra. 'So easy, so mainstream.'

We're all rich now. All we need to do's collect.

'I love you,' Mavra says to me.

'That's too bad,' I say, 'There's something dead about you, Mavra. Something old, ancient, at least. I'm alive, I could go on for ever.'

Later, Mister Wu says I could have been more politic. 'You could at least say 'thanks'',' he says. 'It doesn't cost, it oils the wheel.'

'No, no,' says Mister Han, 'avoid the possibility of doubt.'

'Why should Dex seek out this superbeast?' I ask.

'Do battle with your nemesis,' says Mister Han, who doesn't compromise.

'Identify him, then you bluff,' says Mister Wu, who's used to compromise. How come he's lost his soul at blackjack? 'Or her, of course,' he adds.

'Mavra is one of us,' says Mister Han. 'She has a memory. She knows. She has poor blood. It scrapes, as it goes round. Her feet throb with walking upon stones. You,' he says to me, 'you don't belong alongside. You know being poor as whispers only. A few years, not centuries. Thrown out of bars, is all. Not harassed. Not exhorted, not despised. Waiting for the transformation, for rhythms to begin again. "Eternity", you think. Work. To you, that means other guys who'll work for you, respect you. Love you, follow you, slip you underneath their sheets, hug you all night. You can read, but you don't write. Don't know the value of the word, a single word, done well. No offence, but – you're dandruff. There to be brushed off.'

Mister Wu smiles ingratiatingly, and says, 'Mister Han and I – we deal with whole economies, not messages and sufferings.'

'We need Mavra,' I say, to reconcile. 'Absolutely. She's the one who works the abacus. She keeps the track.'

Mavra says to me, 'I could betray you, or betray Dex.

Find his person with the mask, and let them fight it out. Or take the cash, and run, finance your wanderings. Dex launched you, but you've no respect for him, and less for me.'

It sounds right, for now.

She goes on, 'I had two lovers, now I've none. That evens out, and I'm just what you see.'

'You sound sad, Mavra,' I say, cheering her up. 'It's no better being sad than being happy.'

'I used to dance,' she says, trying to widen the conversation. 'Wu and Han, they're just men without women.'

'Well,' I say, 'for sure they dance. I've seen them. Without women; at the same time, not necessarily together.'

'Being crew, all over everywhere,' says Mavra. 'They have to improvise,' maybe she thinks of being near Košice, not anywhere, with many people.

'Come,' says Mister Han, 'we've money to pick up. And there's lots of people to sort through – the one we want may not even wear the mask. We don't know if he's good or bad. Or she.'

This market that we're in – is this abundance, or the poor, bargaining to eat? It's all been disassembled – there's the intestines, salted snakes hung up like woolly socks, the pigs are greased and stuck, varnished, glazed, eyes in a dish, long bodies hauled in from life classes. Then – everything seems made of paper – here's a Merc, white goods, back hoes and graders – all to turn mush with the first use. I gawp – 'They'll never sell all this ...' and Mavra says, 'Oh, there are dumps, but mostly it gets ate or used in hell, when there are funerals.'

'Let's get on,' says Mister Han. In his hand he has a kind of bowl – for noodles, maybe – we've a contract, that all Holland's given up to growing bean sprouts. Economies of scale, and rationality.

He picks a girl – what long black hair, securely fastened too – and no! It's not a bowl. A mask, an owl – I see the beak, there are no eye- or mouth-holes, and he clamps it on her face, and Mister Wu comes up behind, secures her arms and lifts her up.

'The bird of wisdom,' Mavra says. 'My! What a reputation! No eyes, no mouth, no seeing evil and no speaking it, but maybe hearing everything.'

They take it back – it's 'her', of course – for Dex. 'Here is the creature, Dex,' shouts Mister Han. 'That flies – we flew – and no doubt walks and swims. If not, she'll have to learn.'

'You idiots,' shouts Dex, 'Fuck! What came into your heads? This place is full of *putes*, and all my cash could buy me anyone I want,' and on he rants. The girl is feisty, she will settle down, and titillate the boss, our Dex, then kill him with a knife and go ahead to make two fortunes, like the story says. Or get a mate to cut him up – though that way you can start a dynasty, there's kids and people walled in towers, bricked up in furnaces. We could be free, and I could wander off ...

'That's a princess, for sure,' says Mavra, much

impressed. 'She'll take the empire from old Dex, and double it ...'

How fortunate, it doesn't happen quite this way. No mask, no girl, and no kidnap.

'Settlement. The Wall. That is where we went bad,' says Mister Wu. 'You must take the train, the camel train – escape the laws of bosses, and of physics. Telephones, especially. Don't plant your seeds and wait to see ... Pick as you go – the yellow and the purple plum, the roses for your hair, the wild asparagus, the apple – venerable and sharp.'

'Don't build,' joins in Mister Han, who generally favours sterner life. 'That way beams won't come down on you. Shamans will cure you – churches won't. Nor doctors! There's no eternity – just moving on and out of sight.'

'Yes!' says Mavra, quite entranced. 'Those dirty shacks! The trains that never stop for us. You're right, Wu, and Han. Constant movement. Everywhere, nowhere, a destiny, without a destination. Stop – and they will shut you up, and put you in a class. In a factory. They'll make you love your neighbours – they too, shut in their box, and lusting for your skin.'

'Not many can keep moving,' says Mister Wu. 'You need to have money, and not spend it.'

Here's the market, full of life in cages. Trays of creatures disassembled, fins, wings and trotters. 'What kind of animal?' asks Mavra. 'And why does Dex want it?'

'To be unique. Something real beautiful. Perhaps just to bring us back,' I say.

The passageways of people moving. They walk, don't cover distances, like they're on a loop. Things not edible look out of place. Maybe Dex wants to eat what we bring back. And if we find a girl, put the mask on her – maybe she'll get eaten too.

The lady beckons. Here's an enclave. Aha! Animals – and us, in intimate connect. It's revelation, epiphany: 'Tomb guardians,' shouts Mister Han. Singly, in pairs, raw stone, and painted. 'There's a kind of lion,' Mavra says, entranced – and there it is, a long waxed beard, and tiny wings. But then, you don't want lift off, you want it just to stand. There's pairs, with horns, and tusks, and wings, and some have paws and some have hooves, and some have human faces, scarlet crests.

'Are they alive?' I ask.

The lady pokes one. It seems moribund. She says, 'You don't want them lively. They are guards, they have the job for ever.'

She's not keen to sell, it seems. Mister Wu's convinced. 'This is what he wanted, Dex. It's clear – these can do anything he wants – they swim, and all the rest. But it's indifferent. What they need to do is stand and guard his tomb. He had a special fear of death, the certainty it would occur, despite his cash and having gangs, and territory.'

'It's quite like Dex,' says Mister Han, 'to want a hybrid thing to watch his interests. But we could try a kidnap too – a sweet Miss Wei, in case we've got the other wrong.'

The lady says, 'I have a Wei right here, you could abduct her, but she'll want a contract too.'

'No, no,' says Mavra. 'He has a tomb, a mausoleum – this guy here,' she points at me – 'He dug it out. The shelter, the command post – that will be his tomb. He said – someone will come and cut him up and do for him. That's why he needs these guards, for afterwards. We'll find a Wei, with long black hair, there's lots round where Dex lives ...'

'The Wei that's here,' the lady says, 'she's got black hair. She sees the war, the next, decisive war – she sees it in her sleep. Fly her away from here – she'll maybe off your boss as well, if that's convenient ...' and on she talks.

I say, 'Let's find Miss Wei back there, in Italy, and so we'll save the fare. It's Dex's destiny to predecease me, but the time is immaterial ... all of us can wait.'

'Let's first collect the cash that's owed,' says Mavra. 'In Kazakhstan they're due to park the cars of all the world, of all the universe, among the dunes. That is their destiny. So is paying us what's due, contracted. Dex comes next.'

'Oh,' says Mister Han, 'we have collecting cash in mind. It can be tiresome – Mister Wu is into compromise, I toe a harder line. Between us, everything will be resolved. You two can leave, carry off the guardians – and we shall do the rest.'

It doesn't quite convince. But first, we must select the

animals. The finest ones are painted rock, one has paws, the other hooves, and tiny wings, the faces of philosophers, and spiny crests.

'They're perfect,' Mavra says.

'Intended for me,' the lady says. 'My grave. I'm a character quite like you'd meet in opera – a sale, a gift, it comes with strings, additional weight of destiny. They'd carry with them part of me, my plot. I cannot sell. But maybe, since you plead ...'

'They're beautiful,' says Mavra, as we truck them out. 'They are my motive, my motif, impelling me toward the boss: his death, a ritual assassination – maybe in competition, or cooperation, with Miss Wei, whom we've yet to meet ...'

'Come down from that,' I say. 'Mavra! The story's been set up by Dex, you don't come in. He's interested in his death and after, not who does the deed.'

She's chastened. 'Well,' she says. 'What is this war that people here are sure will come?'

'Of course,' says Mister Wu. 'You change the continents around, and what guys make, how long they live, and what they eat – all that. How many kids, and how much cash each person has ... War is the speciality, been practised and rehearsed in every key and modulation, in symphonies and fragments, for millennia. It is our way, our food, our drug. Sure, it must come, it is the earthquake unbound, unbounded, when you've shifted all the crust. Dex is irrelevant, a mere bandit holed up in a tree. We hear the rumble, it's the war that everyone prepares. All over, everything is organised for marching and for suffering. Meantime, some decorous collecting ... Pack these fellows up!' and he pats the guardians.

I'd trust Mister Han, trust him with my life, if I thought that he was on my side. We go back to Dex, mistrusting one another. The guardians are silent in their crate.

The scene has not much changed. Dex says, 'I thought you'd bring – a pet, perhaps ... a statement for the tourists. These guardians – you didn't mean them as a threat? A presage? The people here are racist, they can't wait to see me underground. Of course, I do my business on the margins, doing what many wouldn't do. Greasing the wheels. You don't expect the guys will thank you – even those who work for you. I sacrifice myself. Look at the damp, the water in the cave ... These guardians – do they work? It's almost worth a try, a burial, to see how loyal they are, the fine upstanding friends they seem.'

It is my task, eliminating water from his lair. It takes a day. Dex says, 'It's quite astounding ...' Then, he asks, 'Now, what's the big picture? What's it all about? Tell me about this war. Will it impact on me? It could be very bad for business, or it could be very good.'

'If you prefer,' says Mister Wu, 'and not to give offence, we have a human animal who'd oil your days. Miss Wei. She's from the North, and East. We'd ship her in – or fly her. Even walk with her ...' but Dex passes his coldeye over us: 'This war. The guys that run them – they don't have rules. I've rules, and so do other business guys.

You lie to me, or cheat or steal – then life is tough for you. But guys outside, the ordinary ones, they fight, they kill quite indiscriminate, they make their bombs, they vote, they dump their bosses, fight some more, then roister in the streets – they don't have rules. Mavra – your crowd have rules. You understand.'

'Oh yes,' she says. 'That's what I'm running from. From spider's nest to spider's nest – that is my destiny.'

'If you're a fly,' says Dex, 'that is the truth. And, Mavra, you just wait for heathen guys to put your desperation into shape. You're weak, like this guy here,' and he points at me, 'can dig and dry – a marvel, but it's limited. Then all he has is feeling good and promising good futures to his mates. What you want, Mavra? To reform me?' and he laughs. 'I've got my fear of death. "Remember, you will die," it says: me today, and you tomorrow. That keeps me humble, but not cowed.'

'That's very good,' says Mister Han. 'Indeed, quite excellent. Now, do you want these tomb guards, or maybe you prefer Miss Wei?'

'Oh, all of them, of course,' says Dex. 'That's a rule too.'

I ask Mavra. 'How do we get this girl, and handle her with kidnap gloves?'

She says, 'That's easy – you must put an ad. A beauty contest, you don't say it's a competition to get fucked. Besides, Dex prefers remote control, not penetration. You charge an entrance fee, and that we take, since Han and Wu have all our cash. Then, when someone called Miss

Wei applies, we snatch her up. The splendid Wei.'

And that we do. How I admire her, Mavra, knowing how it's done.

Miss Wei, the winner, here she is. I say, 'We're your judges. We can judge you.'

'That's too bad,' she says, 'I won, already. Usually you have to walk, and sing and dance.'

'We can all do that,' says Mavra, who doesn't take to her.

'You don't look like I thought, Miss Wei,' I say.

'And you – you don't look at all like you,' she says.

I wonder if she's from a sect. Far from us, and our fears.

'You know, you are a gift for Dex,' I say. 'Just the body. The spirit stays with you.'

'Oh,' she says, 'I know. I'll keep my eyes shut.'

'I like your style,' I say.

'Not style,' she says. 'Anyone can copy that. It's class.'

'Remember,' I say. 'Dex is big in politics. You're his gold coin, you'll circulate. He's green, of course.'

'His birds are black,' says Wei. 'Must be the water. Look how they circle, high above the living things.'

'He's not quite a normal guy,' I say. I'm cautious, thinking of the smell, the skin feel of his hands: 'But he's a notable, big cheese, tall poppy. He'll lift you up, or cast you down, it's quite indifferent. You'll need all your skills.'

She's beautiful, Miss Wei, that long black hair –

securely fastened on. The face – it is a bowl, the eyes are
not quite there, the mouth is painted shut, it seems; the
nose – it doesn't smell things, just keeps the breasts in
harmony, up-down they go, the wind is pumping in and
out ... you watch the show..

'It's all quite changed,' says Mavra. Now I see she's
quite a lumpy country girl. No class: 'It was an error,
bringing gifts and hoping for rewards in turn. He'll never
let us go, and we're complicit for the future now. The
swamp is drying out, the trucks, the people ...'

'Bad news,' shouts Wei. 'Dex so loves us all – he
wants to try out his entombment. A rehearsal. How sad –
I'd want to be the consort Wei, not stuffed down with the
concubines.'

'Those goddam animals,' Mavra shouts. 'They are an
omen; Dex feels he must buck the destiny they portend.'

There's worse. My mission? – tenoned into Dex's
scheme ... And Han and Wu explain, the money's come,
and in a box. The Chinese crew will keep it safe – some is
for roistering, and most for tax.

We're a sextet, standing, facing out, and Dex seems
into Berlioz, a Mefistofeles. Wei does some *Aida*, Han and
Wu – they must be failed suitors out of *Turandot*, and me
and Mavra ... left over from the *Grand Inquisitor*. There is
no sound. Our mouths are dry. There is no great conductor,
all is up to Dex. The guardians of his tomb – their scarlet
crests stand out like flames. You think 'Valhalla'. Those
polluted, wheeling birds, up high ...

'Friends and partners, I'm not dead. It's a rehearsal,

have no fear,' Dex shouts. 'It's just your shades I need for now. You can walk upon the earth, your second lives, your rebirth – call it as you like – nothing is changed. Service is all, it is the proof of love.' He holds Wei under his arm, her little beak pokes out, that's all.

'You know,' says Dex, quite loud. 'Among you guys – I don't see saviours, jugglers, brokers, boxers ... none of you. And looking further – suppose that China doesn't make it? And we have religions, underage guerrillas, all that stuff, and suburbs, suburbs everywhere, greenhouses with gooseberries, and choking smog ... Suppose, my friends, we have all that, for all our lives ... Maybe it's time for us ... to all go down. Ah, the boredom. As the Cajun poet says, "ennui, smoking his hubble-bubble, dreaming of scaffolds ..." And I shall rule, persist beyond the grave. My businesses are always in demand. They're risky, but eternal. Like the sacred books all say, capitalism's the best, or else, the family... And were those guardians a hint?' He turns on us. We're silent. Mister Han and Mister Wu are crying, their failure's hypothesised before the victory. Mavra whispers to me,

'Of course it was a hint – the furniture for graves – a heavy prompt. Capital? Families? The spirit, and the body – ugh! I must keep running, nowhere a refuge ...' and she shudders: 'Or the tomb? Where can I go? I run and run, the paths all double back.'

'Dex,' I say. 'Old friend. Remember. Storks. Frogs. Our days in nature. And you said you'd pre-decease me ... a promise ...'

'Yes,' whispers Wei. 'Get him to cry. I take it bad, on the same day, for me – celebrity and death.'

'Gone, all gone!' says Dex. 'Look at this place, featureless, characterless – a void, with warring clans. As for your death, my friend,' and he kisses me, his tongue – the sticky mucus, and the colour too ... 'It can be arranged, first me, and then you instantaneously, or almost so. The thing is, to conform to logic, plot and unities.'

'Yes, Dex,' I say, 'we could have been a group, a company, on a stage. Just singing, just an instant back. A public, guys that cry, would die for you, not pretending all the macho stuff that hides their impotence ...'

'Now, now!' says Dex. 'Don't be all odd with me. It's orders that I give, and order that I get. Those worthy guys, outside, who try to bring us down – the honest ones, their hands held out, their uniforms, their guns ... and don't they want their permits, and their pills and *putes*?'

'Don't trawl that line,' I say. 'You can't be saved if you're just a business arm of the whole shoot.'

'There is no "saving". Life goes on until it stops. It doesn't double back,' says Dex.

'It's not for what you've done, Dex,' I say. 'It's after your death. And before mine.'

'You want to wander on?' he asks. 'In your disloyalty?'

'It's the animals, Dex,' I say. 'There stands all your attitude. You should observe – the crows. So sage. And so adroit.'

'Loyalty,' he goes on. 'The only possibility. Bigger

than anything. Wu and Han – they know, despite the suffering. That Wei – she talks to other sides – that weakens her position ...'

'She's scared,' I say.

'So are we all,' says Dex. 'Betrayal's not security. and as for animals – no, they're quite too much. You open up another world of pain and the ephemeral.'

'Dex,' says Wei, showing him some tongue. 'Leave me your empire. When you're done. I'll be the dowager, and bury you, secure. Those animals. On guard.'

Dex ignores her.

'Bugs,' he says. 'Real and mechanical. Bugs in your hair, and bugs in your telephone. I'd bring down the government, but what's the point? It's states the thing. Here, we should secede.' He talks on, how it's done, the laws and such. And then the war. 'They need us. The guys from round here, if they're not into pills and trafficking – they're doctors and the like. Of course, the modern things – they have no cure. But you can make a buck – hot mud and needles. There's still money there.' He talks on, he's a map, a globe. The future, its beliefs, its markets ... 'Those birds – they fly away when they have dined. What's interesting is insects. Bugs. Those stay. They have the vision. They will rule the world – no! They already do, of course.'

He's covered in them. Ants and lice, and things with eyes on wires. He wipes his hands on us, and transfers colonies. That's how you recognise his people. From his hands, his breath – in the air they spin like spores, delve in your lungs, your folds, they eat on you, and exercise, and wave their abdomens. We're covered in this primal life.

'This war,' says Mavra. 'How're you going to manage that?'

'They'll never let us go,' says Dex. 'Until we fight. Then, it isn't how to win, it's how to sacrifice. And threats, and stuff from unread books. Some guys in uniform, of course, and videos.'

'No, no,' says Mavra. 'That way, they'll see it's all a scam.'

'Well, you should know, my dear,' Dex says, quite nastily. 'You must have heard about the jargon, jargon of authenticity. It's everywhere, and inescapable. Conviction doesn't enter in. Guys want to live by laws. And I shall lay them down. Start at the beginning, not the end – which we have reached.'

It is an itchy vision, Dex's. It will attract the good, the bad.

Wei says to me, 'Those quite wrong Chinese sorts, still roistering in their sheds – what will they make of this?'

I don't know. I say, 'Dex will do a deal with all the other clans, before he ditches them. If things go bad in China, guys will come and build the city. Maybe if things are good. In any case, there is no place for us.'

'The politics – it's always all the same,' says Wei. 'Business will bring guys in, then they'll invent the stories.'

'Sometimes the stories start off first, and then the

businesses,' says Mavra, anxious to contradict.

'No,' I say. 'The interesting thing is insects. Spreading them around, and cherishing – when you don't know if you should. I bet they don't reciprocate.'

'You're wrong,' says Mavra. 'It isn't about you, and it isn't about me. Dex is his own centrality, he's interested in himself, his place within the universe. Where he is, where he comes from, where he can go, and the insects are the tiniest part, the seeds. They're people, and they're drops, like spittle in the wind. They feed the animals, they live on them, and then the animals they die, the insects eat them, and on you go.'

'We should perhaps leave, before he tries the war,' but Mavra tells of coloured storks from upper Egypt, with bands of red and blue, and statues named and labelled, and of people who've lived underground, and Wei says 'No, no – I won't go, he'll leave it all to me,' and Mavra tells her: beauty queens – they have no realms, their crowns are tin, and if they've kids, they're not princesses, they even spoil the beauty part ...

Mavra and I – we try to leave. It's night, there's trucks, and phosphorescent pools, and single lamps on poles, so bright ...There's razor wire, Russians with lasers plodding round, multi-eyed, and piles of paper sacks for them to guard.

'Mavra may leave, not you,' and there are Mister Wu and Mister Han: they take me back, and Mavra says, 'I'll not forget – one day, I'll come and save you,' but I don't think that's so, though off she goes, looks back ... and

Mister Han holds me quite tight, and says, 'Dex wants you. He's convinced you have a mission, and can give his project gloss. Or maybe he says "class".'

'Why can't I leave?' I ask Dex. 'This war – you've no personnel. Some *putes*, that give *pompini* for five euros ...'

'Aren't you tired of wars for justice?' Dex says. 'For eternal life? Or living clean? Mine will be a metaphor, but metaphors is what they are about – that, and the massacres. Mister Wu and Mister Han – they don't like people leaving. It's their principle. Travel is one thing – leaving the show is quite another.'

'Mavra left,' I say, quite desperate.

'She said she loves you. That means that she'll be back. Didn't you observe the storks? That's how they work. In life, for lifetimes. Mavra – she's a stork. Childless too – and that's a fortune! Once it was revolution, now it's war – that's what guys want. Have it over with and done, although they say they want to win, not fight. Once it was identity that everybody hoped to have – and now that's what you tire of, quick.'

'You're a philosopher,' I say. 'So – let me go. I'm pleading now.'

'You are the architect,' says Dex, quite stern. 'There's nothing built. That means you make the plan. The vision's yours. Now – make it real.'

'No, Dex! I wanted to be loved, and spread it all around, maybe some work, but gently done,' I say.

'That's nonsense. When love was offered, that you didn't want,' says Dex.

'I didn't say it had to be promiscuous. There was an element of choice, though tacit, Dex,' I say.

'Exactly so,' says Dex. 'The place where all love everyone is in this colony,' and he opens out his hand. And are they ants? Or grasshoppers, or larvae that's all heart and wondering what shape to take ...?

'There!' he says. 'That's universal love, and work as well. A pity we won't get there. That's why you have to build – even in metaphors ...' and on he talks, and Wei is dozing in a chair, she doesn't follow, and I say,

'No, Dex! This is eternity you're pointing to,' and Dex cuts in, 'No – it's to stop my fear, and give me gentle, meaningful extinction. And know it's going on and on ...'

'What?' asks Wei suddenly, alert: 'What is this "it", Dex, that's going on, indifferent to me? And where do I come in?'

'We're special animals,' says Dex. 'That means we have a destiny. You must work out what it is, Wei, and then you act.'

Coming down the hill – a line of little boys and girls, in white, and holding lilies. They must be children of another boss.

'Back, back!' shouts Dex, barring their path, flapping his hands.

'It's just a first communion, Dex,' I say.

'I know,' he says. 'If there was Mavra here, she'd know how the spell is taken off. They should go back inside.'

'You'll need a flag,' says Wei. 'If you're a country. I

am good at flags.' We humour her: I say,

'No insects. That would be grotesque.'

'I'm sure they have their own,' says Dex.

'A wolf snapping at a bird that's taking off,' says Wei.

'Too indecisive,' says Dex.

'A frog, jumping on the moon,' I say. 'That would satisfy the space enthusiasts, and the wildlifers.'

'Too ambitious,' says the consort Wei.

'I know,' says Dex. 'The country: and the flag. We want to have her back: we'll call them "Mavra". The country, so she'll know there is a home. And on the flag, her picture, so she'll know where she's to go.'

'That leaves me out,' says Wei, sniffling, turning away.

'Flag debates are all like that,' I say. 'They leave you out. Besides, Mavra'll come for love, and then not find it.'

'Well,' says Dex, 'that happens too.'

It's genius. Much better than the real. 'Mavra'. The new country, dedicated to unrequited love.

'All this is most unwise,' says Mister Han. 'One time, we could have jollied you along. We used to make the country stuff, the thrones and wigs, all that. But now – such gestures ...' And Mister Wu puts in, 'We need to keep ourselves quite flexible. And not just me and Mister Han – the guys down in the sheds ...' and we can hear them now, the karaoke never stops.

'"Mavra",' says the consort Wei, coming to terms: 'As a flag, a country, all those who don't have one, and are fighting – some for centuries, like the Medes, others, well, they come to mind in flocks – maybe they'd all adhere to Mavra. The country that contains them all, all their desires and destinies.'

'Come off it, Wei,' laughs Dex, and Han and Wu are doubled up with glee. 'Don't think about it. Politics is not your game,' and she goes quiet.

We're lying on a ridge, it's dark. Dex has night glasses, I am held by strings, and where I go, Han and Wu come after, though its hard to say they're followers.

'There goes that owl,' says Dex. 'I'd forgot, how flat their faces are. Not like a bowl. How big those eyes.' He turns to me. 'You know why they're the bird of wisdom?'

'No,' I say. I don't much care.

'It's not their tiny brains,' says Dex, 'it's their neck. They can turn their head right round, and see who's coming up behind – knives, or garrotting wire.'

'Dex, Dex,' I shout. 'Look over there – the cops! They're taking guys and putting them in automobiles.'

'I know,' says Dex. 'I shopped them. They're Frattali. I told you I was into politics. That's how I get to use the Mavra flag ... There – the owl got lucky! How those little things, the mice ... hear how they squeak. Justice – when it comes, it's heavy on you. Then it flies off and lands on someone else. My people – they will see that justice is done, and not to us.'

'You're sure you have these "people", Dex?' I say: 'It seems deserted here.'

'Oh well,' he says, 'that owl is quite anomalous, it's

true – but I can't give advice. Not about where to hunt. I show the way that things are going to be – and after me, the silence, or the talons. Not my domain. Not mine to interfere.'

The owl flies off, making noises like a train. 'Go, go,' says Dex, philosophically. 'Leave us with the guardians. They don't tell anything we didn't know. All my efforts with the animals – we haven't learned.'

'You're sure that's what they're for,' I ask. 'To teach?' and Mister Wu makes hungry sounds behind.

'If we have purposes,' says Dex, 'they must have them too. Or – if it's just mechanical, the talk of justice is air breathed in, and out.'

The sign says: 'Free country of Mavra. Documents issued.'

'Wei wanted to say "Welcome". But that attracts the wrong sort,' Dex says.

'Those Senegalese ...' I say.

'They have a country,' Dex says. 'This is for those without. We'll even tattoo a number on. It's transit for storks and wolves – and the passage is quite free. "Enter, and be saved." That's what it means, that's what you need.'

'Those people come and work for you, Dex,' I say, noncommittal.

'You were such a pain,' he says: 'First you wanted work, and now it's hmmmm ... Saved – you can take that any way. You should.'

It's like we're in the hide again. Now, he asks me, 'Is

your mission any clearer? My respect for you increases. Not liking you, though.'

'I've always felt I am a special person,' I say.

'We all do,' says Dex. 'Where do you come from?'

'You mean parents? Cities? Experiences?'

'No, no,' he says. 'I mean like – I know about the revolution, drugs, religion, freedom and ecstasy. There's been lay priests, and guitarists: lots of those, and singers too. Then there was Engels – he showed there's a motor in it all – the plants, the animals. It tells us how things will work out – the physics, the right way. So – how's it been with you?'

'Right now,' I say, 'I feel hemmed in. Fulfil the past, and open up the future ...'

'Yes, well,' says Dex. 'Maybe you could write it down.'

Mister Han and Mister Wu – they don't join in.

Of course, 'Well, there's Proust,' I say, remembering Mavra. 'That's a way you really get to know people.'

'Oh, people,' says Dex. 'Knowing them in stories – that's so easy.'

Are there animals in Proust? They don't have stories. Does that mean you never know them? Mister Han and Mister Wu – they didn't learn from books, it seems. They must have stories, but they don't tell us. They know all about us, and they don't let that out, either.

'Mavra' is a lean country. 'They let it happen because no one cares,' says Mister Wu. 'Another country doesn't count.' It makes no difference to him, nor to Mister Han.

Dex's bunker – that is sparse. I hear a disc – jolly enough, *Les veuves de la Coulée*, it goes on and on, vinyl, I guess. The widows go to town to buy bright fabrics for new knickers. There's two little pigs. Pecaries, in a corner. Dex says, 'The bastards shot the sow. These two – I must protect them.' They scramble about.

Wei doesn't like the setup. I stand outside, and hear her working up a scene: 'Those pigs! Pigs in the house – is this your country? This is it?' Dex mumbles, then he shouts, he tries to shout her down.

'This business,' Wei is shouting. 'The burying. Bodies – and now these pigs. Maybe the bodies are the pigs, and the pigs are guys you didn't like?'

'It's loyalty,' shouts Dex. 'A thing that's alien to you. Protecting those who need it, and don't ask. The business – is just business, and everyone but you, they understand it. It's not a kingdom, and there is no queen, no will, no patrimony.'

'I never knew they were so intimate,' says Mister Han.

Wei is screaming now, and Dex says she's a virus, but he will wash his hands and wear a mask, and maybe they will find a cure for her. We see her darkly whirling round.

There's general noise, and shooting too. 'Oh no,' says Wei; she comes outside and sees us: 'Oh, I'm so confused...'

'Just say who paid you,' says Mister Han.

'I was so sure they didn't shoot the sow. She came back – I saw her nosing round. I was afraid,' says Wei, improvising.

'We've all a destiny, or else a vision, one or other.'
Mister Wu is cool, he says, 'Dex had his destiny. Who has
the vision? It doesn't seem like Wei has one, though her
aim is good ...'

Dex looks quite bad, shot up.

'The trouble is,' says Mister Wu, '"Mavra" doesn't
have a hospital. Usually the people who are hit here don't
go to one.'

'I told you I'd go first,' Dex says to me. 'Make this
my tomb, and set the guardians on watch. Don't have
consort Wei buried alongside. And feed the little pigs.'

The smell fron Dex is like the hide, on that first day.
It's boar.

'They're from Romania,' says Dex. 'They ship them
in, and shoot them.'

A trail, or a parade, of little things is quitting Dex's
pantleg. 'They know!' he says. 'But promise me, that
when I'm gone, you'll build the city-state, our "Mavra".
Maybe a hospital or two, although it might not save me ...'
We say we'll build, but know we won't.

'Those little pigs are lapping up the blood,' says Wei.

'It's a good sign. There isn't much. He is almost
better,' says Mister Wu, but Dex is fraught, beyond the
lies. He says,

'Well, they can have my blood. Don't let them eat the
rest.'

Wei says, 'It was just nothing, I just fooled around,
some pirouettes, and there's this thing – it's called a pistol,

I believe, it sounded quite like castanets, I never meant to end the show ...'

But Dex is going where he won't come back.

'I much regret the storks and frogs,' he says. 'They should have worked it out. But maybe there's some pig in me, and now some me in them. And with those animals outside to guard the tomb ...' It's sad, we cry. We wish it would end quick. Dex says,

'I could have been a swine, enjoyed myself, and others too. Some bosses are like that, with massacres and special laws, forests for orgies, hunting with dogs ... And I was modest, quite the Jansenist.'

'*Je ne suis pas ton ennemi,* Dex,' I repeat.

'No, you never forsook me,' he says. 'Whatever crap I handed you.'

Mister Han and Mister Wu edge to the exit. 'We'll get those tomb guards into place,' whispers Mister Wu.

'Those pecaries,' says Mister Han – 'You want them in as sacrifice, or out?'

'Oh no!' says consort Wei, 'They're quite so cute! We'll let them run away.'

'Bring down the curtain,' Dex shouts out. 'Bring down the roof. It's finished! This guy—' and he points to me, 'will do the sequel.'

Our arms are raised. We tire, we drop them. Dex goes on, 'I always did my best for them, the animals. The insects too – one day we'll eat them in a pie,' and he laughs. 'Among the worst, I was the best. And now,' and he grips my hand, 'This guy knows little about traffic, buying and selling, all what turns the world. It's up to him...' and on he goes.

'No regrets, Dex. Those make a leaden drop, where you will be,' I say.

'I had beliefs and fears,' he says. 'The fears predominate, and rightly so.'

'I didn't know you had beliefs,' I say.

'You bastards!' Dex shouts. 'Eating at my table. A bit of digging! Letting other scum do all the work! I believe in destiny, what's coming. Often it is written down.'

Who can't believe in destiny?

We drop the roof. It makes a mound.

The tomb looks good. The noble guards stare on. No one's around who wants to dig Dex up.

Wei says to me, 'Maybe – if I took my clothes off, you'd be in a more forgiving mood?'

'It's possible,' I say. 'I'm sure it's worked before.'

'Well,' says Mister Han, 'the trades go on. "Mavra" is ever more autonomous.'

'Can it last?' asks Mister Wu. 'No one seems to care. Another country – only we Chinese have doubts. The creatures – they just jig about. The guardians – they just stare.'

'The next guy, the one that's coming in,' says Wei. 'Is not so soft as Dex.'

'The story's changed, if that is what you knew,' I say. 'You plotted for an "afterwards". You'd maybe better put your clothes back on.'

'Hey, guy,' she shouts, 'I'm not a *pute*!'

'Of course, it is the thought that counts,' I say.

'My!' she shouts again – 'How full of things banal and commonplace you are! Dex now – he could charm with words, but you! Your empty project! Never specified.'

'I've no work,' I say to her. 'I'm desperate again. Wei – you can always do your work. Now, we should sort out the animals. It's useless only having those who eat each other. Let's make space for some compassion here.'

'That's incredibly sexist,' Wei says, angry. 'About the work. When I'm thirty, no one will give me work. Besides, Dex thought the storks were useful. He said they brought the babies. Probably because he couldn't perform the four-leg dance with me. The stupid guy.'

'That's sexist, Wei!' I say. 'Incredibly! Dex had deep thoughts, I'm sure, that stopped him jigging ... Wu and Han! – put up some signs – that here's a sanctuary, for flowers, nonhuman things. The flowers are beautiful, and they come back each year, not like you, Wei, or me ...'

'We would do that,' says Mister Wu, 'but we can't write like they do here.'

'Do it anyway,' I say, There may be tourists here ...'

Mister Wu and Mister Han, they do it, the sign. My only command.

'It says, "Danger. Mines",' says Wei. 'That may be all they know.'

What shall we do now? The Chinese crew – will they get to build the city? Surely, that's dead, like Dex. The new boss – the 'stern father', he calls himself. Much deeper into politics – will he inherit Wei? Will Wei inherit him?

'Pity? Understanding?' asks Mister Wu. 'Why?'

The new boss takes the board down that says 'Mavra', City of Mavra. Republic. Sanctuary. So, no country, no war. 'I do things quite differently,' the new boss says. 'I'm deeper into politics.'

And it seems, not only no country, no war – the board is taken down, 'Mavra' disappears – and Mavra, the real Mavra, reappears.

'My!' she says. 'How many people there are out there,' and she waves a hand, to everywhere not here, where she has been, travelling.

Later, she says to me, 'I still love you – but I'm lucky, there is nothing from your side.'

'Well, would you expect a story to help, or the animals to show you something?' I ask, quite irritated.

Mavra says, 'Of course they help. But I don't need help, and they won't help you, my love.'

We talk a bit about Dex, his vision. 'He was a fearful guy, if you weren't loyal,' says Mavra. 'And didn't do his work.'

'It's good to have you back,' I start. She smiles, not much response. She says,

'This new guy – he's a niggler. Organisation, is his thing. And loyalty, of course.'

'That's good,' I say. 'He could have been a crazy, on the dope, and crazy twice.'

'It's not so good,' she says. 'He doesn't think you're

loyal. Too close to Dex, and his wild zoo.'

'It wasn't sentiment with Dex,' I say. 'Nostalgia, for the swamps, the skinny-dipping with the crocs. He wanted an Acadia, built here, and beautiful.'

'We all want something like,' she says. 'And boast about it, screw anyone who isn't up for it.' I see the new guy – just one time. He's got the guardians from the tomb, stolen, cleaned. And as for Wei – he doesn't look the type who'd give a girl the best of times.

'I guess I'll try you out,' he says. 'You don't look good for much.' I see that Dex is on his mind. Profaning tombs – I guess that is this new guy's line. 'I'd say you need to try elsewhere,' he says, 'But wandering off – who knows what secrets you may have?'

'Oh,' I say, 'I've secrets, certainly. And that is what they'll stay. I'm not into writing down and broadcasting.'

Maybe he doesn't grasp, behind that face banal, he keeps his brain quite schtum. 'Loyalty,' he says: 'That's the first step. There are no more. Doing what you're asked, is all.' It's a bad sign. The animals – you don't get much from asking them, nor loyalty without reward.

Later, I say to Mavra, 'My dear – I think I don't fit in. It seems I mustn't leave, and shouldn't stay.'

'Yes,' she says. 'You should have come with me.'

'But you've returned,' I say, 'so I'd have doubled back, and faced this threat, and missed the death of Dex.'

'You will be missed,' she says, 'by Mister Wu, but not by Mister Han.'

'This new boss – if he tries to wipe me out, I shall

resist,' I say.

She says, that's what they say and do, the guys in my position.

'I wouldn't want a tomb like Dex,' I say. 'Just put my body on the ground, and let them feast – the wolves, the little flying things. Let it scatter, into everything. Those guardians – they're not up to it, they don't protect. And you, Mavra, what will you do for me, when all this comes about?'

'Oh,' she says, 'I'll wash your body.'

'And say the things they say?' I ask.

'Exactly so,' she says.

About the author

John Fraser has lived in Rome since 1980. Previously, he worked in England and Canada.

www.ingramcontent.com/pod-product-compliance
Lightning Source LLC
Chambersburg PA
CBHW030315180626
46810CB00003B/1081